Face at the Edge of the World

Also by Eve Bunting

Someone Is Hiding On Alcatraz Island

Face at the Edge of the World

Eve Bunting

Clarion Books
TICKNOR & FIELDS: A HOUGHTON MIFFLIN COMPANY
New York

Clarion Books
Ticknor & Fields, a Houghton Mifflin Company
Copyright © 1985 by Eve Bunting

Library of Congress Cataloging in Publication Data
Bunting, Eve, 1928–
Face at the edge of the world.
Summary: Haunted by the suicide of a gifted young
black writer who was his best friend, Jed pursues the
reason for it.
[1. Suicide — Fiction.   2. Afro-Americans — Fiction]
I. Title.
PZ7.B91527Fac   1985   [Fic]   85-2684
ISBN 0-89919-399-4

s 10 9 8 7 6 5 4 3 2 1

For Christine and Richard,
with my love and thanks

Face at the Edge of the World

1

I've heard older people say they will always remember where they were the day they heard John Fitzgerald Kennedy was assassinated. I wasn't even born then, and my father would have been only about my age. But now I understand what those people meant. I will always remember where I was when I heard that my best friend, Charlie Curtis, had committed suicide.

It was early on a Monday morning in May, and I was cycling to school. I'd be meeting Annie at the corner of Hudson and Loma Linda Drive, and we'd walk or ride the last few blocks to Oceanside High (O-Hi) the way we've done every morning for the past two and a half months, since we started what my father sneeringly refers to as "going together."

My heart was pumping as I pedaled on Hudson through the outskirts of the crummy residential area where Dad and I live, past the rinky-dink markets, and the used-clothing shops with their dusty windows, and the dry cleaners advertising their dollar-a-garment specials. And I was hurrying, so I'd be there before her, so I could watch her coming. It wasn't the hurrying though, or the effort on the hill that was making my heart pump to bursting. It was the thought of being with Annie.

It's funny about us.

I don't know what she sees in me. She's gorgeous and smart and rich, and I'm nothing special. And then there's another thing. How did I get this feeling so suddenly? Annie's been in school with me for three years. I knew her. I talked to her. I must have looked at her, and I must have seen her. But how could I have? If I'd looked at her and seen her, I'd have fallen in love with her long ago. I'm almost sure I love her now. But it's hard to be certain. Maybe at seventeen you're not supposed to be certain.

So I was pedaling along, thinking about love and Annie, which for me is the same thing, and I was thinking how spring in California has to be the best time of all, except maybe for summer, and I saw a bunch of kids from O-Hi standing on the sidewalk in front of the 7-Eleven. There was something weird about the way they were clumped there, as if they were holding a meeting. They stood so still, not horsing around the way we usually do when there's a bunch of us together. And then it was as if they saw me, as if they'd been expecting me. As if they were waiting.

For some reason, I slowed.

When I got closer I could see who was there, Duane Watson, Bob Rothman, some of the other seniors, and a couple of eleventh graders, too. I glided the last few yards to the curb.

"What's happening?" I nodded toward the newspaper Bob was holding. "Somebody drop the bomb or something?"

2

"You don't know?" Duane's skinny and pale, and he has an Adam's apple as big as a baseball. He was having some kind of trouble speaking. The lump in his throat moved soundlessly up and down, up and down, and I thought, Shoot! Maybe they *did* drop the bomb, no kidding! I got off the bike and stood holding on to it.

"It's Charlie Curtis," Duane said.

"What about him?"

"He's dead." Bob pushed the newspaper at me.

I laughed. "What do you mean, dead? God, for a minute I thought the end of the world had come."

"He's *dead*," Glenn Ponderelli said.

"You mean . . . he lost his scholarship? What?"

"*Dead*, man! As in deceased, defunct, croaked! Are you stupid or something?" Glenn's fists were clenched as if he wanted to hit somebody, and his face was scrunched up and twisted.

They were all watching me. I thought of the day Annie and I biked out to Beldon Farms and we were sitting in a field and cows came and stood silently staring.

"Charlie hanged himself. Saturday night in his garage. His mother found him." Bob shoved the paper under my nose.

"Hanged himself? Charlie?" This must be some kind of joke. But they wouldn't joke about this. I licked my lips. "You're kidding, aren't you?"

Bob shook his head. "It's all here, in the paper. It was on the radio, too. It took them a couple of seconds to get to the name, and we were having breakfast and we about freaked out. 'Promising student at Oceanside High?' Man! And then they said his name. I couldn't believe it! My mom ran out and brought the *Sentinel* in from the porch, and there it was."

I took the paper from him and tried to focus on it.

3

"The *Sentinel* sure picked up on the story fast," Glenn Ponderelli said. "How do you figure they got the picture and everything so quick?"

"Aw, they had it already," Bob told him. "They had all the publicity stuff because of the scholarship."

The photograph in the paper jumped out at me. I'd taken it. I'm photographer for the yearbook and sometimes I cover school stuff and sports for the *Sentinel*. I'd taken this when Charlie published his second story. OUR BUDDING BEST-SELLING AUTHOR the caption had read. Now it said: CHARLIE CURTIS DEAD. There he was, grinning up at me, the way he'd grinned that day. "I'm so-o-o black and I'm so-o-o beautiful," he'd cooed, making kissing sounds at me. "And you're so-o-o white and so-o-o ugly." And all the time I'd been saying, "Stay real, man. This is serious. Try to look like a budding best-selling author." In the picture he still grinned.

But now he was dead. And the thought came to me suddenly that I hadn't seen Charlie grin like that in a long time.

"It has to be a mistake," I said.

"No mistake, Jed. Read it."

It was all there, the way Bob had said. My eyes and my mind worked in jumps, skipping sentences, understanding some of what I saw, some of it going through my head with no comprehension at all. He'd been pronounced dead at 10 P.M. Sunday — His mother was taken to the hospital, suffering from shock . . . later released — He'd sold two stories . . . one won the Junior Literary Achievement Award . . . scholarship to UC at Santa Barbara.

I blinked, seeing plain as plain Charlie's excited face the day he found out about that scholarship.

"It could have been tailor-made for me, Jed. Listen to

this. 'Interested in Literary Achievement. High moral character.' " I'd rolled my eyes, and he'd lifted a hand and pretended to chop me.

"And get this, Jed. 'Preference will be given to the son or daughter of a practicing minister of religion.' " He'd beamed at me. "You know my dad. When he's not pruning trees, he's pruning and preaching for the Lord."

Charlie'd applied for scholarships to a bunch of UC campuses, but as soon as he got that acceptance to Santa Barbara the decision was made. We'd shaken hands. "You and me, bro. The old Gemini men, together again."

Charlie! Charlie! You were so happy then. What happened? I rustled the *Sentinel* and made myself go on reading.

"...survived by his parents, Mr. and Mrs. Ronald Curtis, a younger sister, Evelyn, and a younger brother, David, active in Pony League baseball."

I stood, looking at the picture of Charlie, and then I let my glance slide away, and I saw his face again grinning at me from behind the glass of the red newspaper rack on the sidewalk, and I stared back down at the paper in my hand.

"But why did he do it?" I asked. "They didn't say *why?*" My voice had started to shake, and I saw my hands had started too. I folded the *Sentinel* to hide Charlie's smile, careful not to put the crease across his face.

Duane shrugged. "Who the hell knows why? Could be he *did* lose the scholarship. But why would he care? Somebody'd be sure to give him another one."

"Could be he was doing dope," Glenn offered, but my glare shut him up.

I thought it was Bob who muttered, "Maybe even Charlie didn't know why he did it. Maybe he just *did* it!"

Everything was so strange, as if we were under water,

faces blurred, words coming from a distance. I held out the folded paper. "Whose is this?"

Bob took it. "Are you OK, Jed?"

I nodded.

"Want me to buy you one of the papers? I've got a quarter right here."

"No. Thanks." I must have put the kickstand down, because I had to knock it up before I could get back on my bike.

A voice called after me, "You heading on to school?" I didn't answer. I didn't know where I was going.

But, of course, I was going to Annie.

I pedaled, the sun warm on my back, thoughts mushing inside my head. No friend now to go with to Santa Barbara. What would we do about the apartment? We'd paid two months rent. It was going to be great. I'd be at Brooks Institute on my photographic scholarship; he'd be at UC at Santa Barbara on his fine-arts one. Two all-time lucky dudes! Weekends we could make the trip back, both of us on Charlie's motorbike. If we got up early enough, we'd easily cover the distance north to Oceanside and have two good days. He'd drop me off at Berkeley to meet Annie, who was starting there in the fall. Then he'd buzz on home and see Dominique, who still has a year of high school to go.

I crammed on my brakes and dragged my feet on the pavement. Dominique! Did she know? Oh, God! Maybe *she'd* heard it on the radio or gone out for the *Sentinel* and seen Charlie, Charlie's face.... My heart was pounding. Had she had any idea that he was going to do this? Was it because of her? Had they ... had she, decided to call it quits, tired of the sneaking around and the lies?

No. She'd have found some way to stop him.

I pedaled again, slowly, head down. I had a quick flash of Charlie's garage, the open rafters that crossed the roof. We stored our surfboards up there when it was too cold to hit the waves. I saw the boards: mine blue with the lightning bolt, Charlie's yellow. Not too many black guys surf, I don't know why. Charlie used to kid about it. "We can't swim, didn't you know that, white boy? Heavy muscles." He'd grin that sudden, startling grin.

Where had he slung the rope? Did he have to move the boards? It was spidery in the rafters. One time Charlie squashed a black widow and dropped it on me.

Where did he get the rope, anyway? His dad kept a bunch of old odds and ends in a metal trunk. There could have been a piece in that. It would have had to be long, though. And strong. There was a funny sound, like a bee droning past my ears, and I realized it was me, moaning. Charlie! Why did you do it? Why?

Now I could see the corner, and Annie waiting. I saw her bright blue windbreaker and her hair dropping straight and black to her shoulders.

I was sweating, my hands slipping on the handlebars. The bike wheels crunched over dead magnolia leaves, sent pods skittering under the tires.

I pulled up beside her.

Annie pushed her hair back with one finger the way she always does, first behind one ear, then behind the other. It fell forward again the way it always does. It makes me laugh when she does that. "Futility, futility," I say, and I pull the sides all the way across her face. She shakes it back and laughs, too.

"Oh, Jed!" she said, and I could tell she knew. I could tell by her voice and by the wetness on her cheeks.

"I called you," she said. "There was nobody there."

"My dad's away on a job. Oh, God! Annie!"

"I called Dominique, too. She knew already. She's not coming to school. She told her dad she's sick."

"She probably is."

I dropped my bike and Annie dropped hers, and we ran toward each other and hugged, and we were both crying. Crying for Charlie.

2

"Annie, I've got to go see his mom — I can't just..." The sentences wouldn't finish for me. My thoughts darted like lizards.

Annie was still holding me. "Do you want me to come?"

"Uh-uh." I freed myself from her arms. "Thanks, Annie. But I've got to go by myself. I don't know if I'll make it back to school or not."

She nodded, and I felt her standing there as I cycled away.

I tried to make my mind numb as I rode along because I knew if I could it would be easier, like novocaine before they drill on a tooth. But Charlie kept pushing himself back into my thoughts. More novocaine. Please. I can still feel, and it hurts like hell.

And what do you say to the mother of somebody who's killed himself? You can't mouth off stuff like "Gee, it was too bad about Charlie!" or "Please accept my sympathy." I slowed, the novocaine working so good now that I couldn't come up with words that were even halfway possible.

And then, when I got to Charlie's street, I saw that there was a police car in his driveway, and I quickly rode on past, made a U-turn and hauled back around. There was no point in trying to talk to Charlie's mother when the cops were there.

What now? I didn't want to go to school, where everybody would be asking questions. But I didn't want silence either, the stuffy quiet and emptiness of our bungalow in Canterbury Court. At least in school I'd have the comfort of Annie.

The bell had to have rung already for first period when I got there, but the halls were still jammed with kids. Some of the girls were crying.

I walked quickly because I didn't want anybody to stop me or say anything. Not responsible for my actions. Leave me alone. Just don't ask.

D D Hysinger and Monk and the rest of the dopers were standing together, up by the door to the computer lab. One of them peeled off when he saw me. He's a freshman, Lon somebody, and he was weaving as he came down the hall. When he stopped in front of me, I tried to dodge around him, but there was no way.

"Geez, I'm real sorry about Curtis," he mumbled. "He was a nice guy. But you know something?" He leaned closer and lowered his voice. The smell of his breath was sickening. Maybe I'd puke on his feet and that would move him.

"*I* saw her face," he said. "Maybe he saw it too. Maybe that's why he did it."

I jerked my head back, away from the fumes. "You mean Charlie? Whose face did he see?"

"Hers." He shook his head, and the silver marijuana leaf he wore on a chain shivered against his neck. His eyes were

10

hazy, dulled by booze, or dope, or whatever he was full of.

"Her face was nice," he said, and turned and began weaving away.

"Whose?" I called. "Wait a second."

The PA system crackled, filled with static. I wondered if I should go after him. Anything that guy said had to come straight out of space, but still.

"Attention, students. Attention."

It was Mrs. Carruthers, the principal, asking us all to please go to our classes, and when she finished squawking, I looked to see where Lon was, but he'd disappeared.

Annie sits four rows in front of me in English lit and two seats over. Today she sat half-turned, and I knew she was watching for me. When she saw me slip into my seat, she smiled, and her smile was so sweet it almost made my tears start. I wished she and I were out of here. But out of here would be just as bad. There wasn't anywhere to go to leave this behind. I tried to smile back so she'd know I was OK.

When Mr. Brown came in, he let his eyes wander up and down the rows, taking mental attendance or maybe just checking us out. His glance slowed on me, stopped for a second on Charlie's empty desk.

"You all know the sad news," he said. "Charlie Curtis is dead." He paused. "I'm not going to give you any bull about how he's gone to a better life. Charlie's life was good here. He had friends. He had a loving family. He had talent." Head bent, Mr. Brown fussed with a paper on his desk. "All gone."

Yeah, all gone, I thought. You were supposed to write the stories, Charlie, and I was going to take the pictures. *The Atlantic Monthly*," you said. " '*The New Yorker*.' We'll only work for the best." Except '*The New Yorker*' didn't use photographs. I rubbed my fingers across the bony ridge above my eyes.

Mr. Brown was reading something from a book of poems. I only half heard it. It was about nothing being broken but the body, nothing lost but breath. I guess it was beautiful, but it didn't make much sense to me. If your body's broken and your breath's lost, what's left?

I wrote *LON* and drew a square around it. I'd find him later. Charlie couldn't have been into drugs with that bunch, could he? Not Charlie. I was doodling in my notebook mindlessly, circles and squares, filling them in, adding legs, adding arms, turning them into Gemini men. Gemini men are Charlie's and my secret signals — *were* our secret signals. Everything I wrote or drew was blurred.

Charlie had seemed preoccupied for a while. I'd noticed it, I remembered, and I'd let it go. I was too busy with Annie, with thoughts of her and me. Too busy figuring my moves. Sometimes Charlie did drift off anyway, when he was working on a story. "Coming up with a plot line," he'd call it, though personally I never saw much plot in any of his stories. They were usually about strange people with mixed-up feelings doing mixed-up things that I guess were significant. I never really understood them. Sometimes, when I finished one, I wondered if Charlie had those kinds of thoughts and feelings himself. If he had, he did a good job of hiding them. But I always knew that he wasn't on drugs. Not Charlie.

Unbidden, my camera eye focused on the garage, the rope, the hanging body, and I quickly clicked the lens cap on and cut into darkness. Oh God! Please don't let me think about that.

The girl in front put her hand behind her back, wiggled it, and passed me a note from Annie.

12

"Let's buy some lunch and go up to Chitney Trail. OK? A."

She'd know we couldn't get up there and back over lunchtime, so we'd be cutting afternoon classes. Annie would miss swimming, and I'd have to skip Noah's photo lab. I don't miss Noah's lab for anything. I'd never have had the scholarship if it weren't for Noah. But today was a different day, and this wasn't just anything. Annie was looking around, and I nodded.

She was at the bike racks before me, and we pushed through the kids in the parking lot and out onto Loma Linda. O-Hi doesn't have a cafeteria. The park across the street is always jammed at lunchtime, and the red snack truck that parks by the gates does a roaring business. So does the 7-Eleven. Even though it's farther away, it's usually faster. I got in line while Annie stood by the empty newspaper racks and watched the bikes. I don't think I ever remember a time when those racks were empty, when the *Sentinel* was sold out by lunchtime.

Behind the 7-Eleven counter, Big Eddie was talking about Charlie. "He did it Saturday night, you know. They were all away."

I closed my eyes. He'd hung there all alone, a night and a day.

"I heard he left a note," somebody said.

"Yeah, but a woman who was in this morning told me it didn't say much. Just good-bye."

I found a wad of tissues in my pocket, and my fingers pulled it apart.

Eddie Jr. came in from the back room. That's where he stays mostly. Eddie Jr.'s not exactly retarded, but for sure he's not totally with it.

"Hi, Jed," he called to me. His head flops to one side, and it's hard not to flop your own when you're talking to him.

"Hi, Eddie."

"I liked Charlie," he said.

"I know you did, Eddie. Charlie liked you too."

"Charlie never called me loony tunes."

"I know, Eddie." Criminy, I was going to bawl in a minute. There's nothing like a semiretarded kid looking at you with big mournful eyes to choke you up. I held on.

When I got to the head of the line, Big Eddie said, "I'm real sorry, Jed," and I nodded. It seemed as if he was going to say more, but maybe the look on my face stopped him.

I paid for two sandwiches, two apples and two cartons of milk, and Eddie Jr. put them in a sack. His father had to tell him not to put the sandwiches in the bottom. He has to tell him that all the time. I stashed everything in my book bag and kept my change and Annie's separate.

It was warm outside, the sun high in the sky. We cycled along Loma Linda without talking. Annie was ahead of me, her long black hair streaming out behind. She stood on the pedals, leaning forward as the hill to Chitney Trail got steeper, and I looked at her rear end in the tight jeans, at her legs that I knew were long and silky, all of her long and silky, and I remembered lying in bed this morning thinking about her. Lusting after her, more like.

I'd lain there debating whether or not I should ask her to come home with me after school. My father had gone. He'd be living in his camper, and he wouldn't be back for a month, at least. Most of the Callahan jobs take that long. They put up maybe a hundred houses, and it takes the painting crew a few weeks to go in behind them and roll the walls. My father's a charter member of that painting crew.

14

I'd been in my bed in my room that's no bigger than a jail cell, in our "bungalow" that's not much bigger than a doghouse, and I'd turned on my squeaky mattress and heard Mr. Yamamoto next door cough and spit his morning spit and I'd heard his morning splash into the toilet bowl, and I'd thought, I can't bring Annie here. Not perfect, shining Annie. Not ever. She's seen the outside as we've cycled by and that's bad enough. I'd flipped an airy hand toward "the old homestead." But no way would I ever bring her in.

I watched her riding in front of me now, and I was thinking how I'd gotten up this morning a whole hour early and how I'd shoveled all the papers and junk out of the living room, just in case. How I'd taken the throw-away ads and the junk mail my father keeps till it's yellow and mildewed and piled them all on the back porch, and how I'd run our ancient vacuum over the rug and changed the sheets on my bed. Just in case. Sure, just in case. Now, biking up the slope, I was thinking, too, that when I put on those sheets, and when I was doing all that wishing and lusting, Charlie was already dead. God!

Annie turned off onto the rough, earth-packed path that led between the redwoods to Chitney Meadow. She looked over her shoulder at me and shouted, "Come on, slow-poke."

Then the trees spread out, and we got our first glimpse of the stripe of blue ocean in the distance; the clearing began and then the wide spread of grassland.

We walked, pushing the bikes, stopping at the fallen log that has the view down across the dry scrub and the manzanita and the patches of purple wild flowers. A hawk hung high on pointed wings. We stayed away from the edge. It's better to take in the whole sweep of the view and not look too closely at what's been thrown down from the sheer drop to the dump below. Old, rusted beer cans. Cheez-It bags. Used condoms. The sun glittered on shards of glass from broken wine bottles. "The Edge of the World," the kids call it. "Just toss it over the Edge of the World," they say. And everyone does.

We laid the bikes down and sat on the log, and Annie put her hand in mine. She held her face to the sun. "I can't believe it yet."

"I know. I wonder how long it takes for it to sink in?"

Annie pushed her hair back. "Maybe we should make copies of what Brown said this morning and give them out. The words were nice."

"A kind of memorial," I said, and we sat for a long time not talking, and I choked up again.

After a while we ate our lunch and drank our lukewarm milk. "I should have bought juice," I said. "There's nothing worse than hot milk."

"It's OK."

We packed the crumpled paper and cartons in the sack, and I stowed it in my book bag and then we stood up. Annie bent to brush the scaly bits of log off her jeans, and I saw a piece she'd missed, and I touched her and then we were clinging together, kissing and stroking. I pushed my hands under her hair to the softness of her neck, and everything inside me was overflowing with my need for her. She'd taken off her jacket, and I could feel her, all of her, the heat from her body coming through the cotton of her shirt. Her breath fanned my cheek.

"Annie! Annie!" My fingers moved across her shoulders, fumbled with the buttons on her checked shirt.

"Don't, Jed. Please." Her hands covered mine, and I stepped back a pace, listening to the raggedness of my breath. I looked at her eyes, a little slanted, dark as her hair, her skin creamy and soft as close-woven silk.

16

"What is she ... Jap?" Dad had asked once after he'd seen us in a movie line.

"Hawaiian," I'd told him. "One set of grandparents."

He'd sniffed. "Jap!"

Annie smiled shakily at me and laid her hand against my cheek. "You look so mean all of a sudden. Did I ever tell you that that mean look of yours is a real turn-on?"

"My mean look? I didn't know I had one." I moved my lips against her hand.

"You do. Your eyes have ... this kind of hard blueness. But then you look at me, and it's as if a door opens. You let me in, and you keep everyone else out. I feel so special."

I was a little surprised that Annie knew me so well. I do keep people out. Probably just about everyone except Annie and Mrs. Sanchez ... and Charlie. And I'd never even let them in all the way. I don't know why that is. Or maybe I do ...

Annie's smile widened. "Of course, there are one or two other things about you that turn me on too."

We were holding each other tightly again and then for no reason Charlie slid back into my head. I let go of Annie and picked up her jacket. Charlie was lying, stiff and cold somewhere, probably in the Sunset Mortuary, and here I was, his best buddy, trying to get it on with Annie! I felt lousy.

"It's OK, Jed. If Charlie can see us, he's saying it's OK too. You know he is."

I shook out the jacket. "Maybe. And maybe I don't know as much about Charlie as I thought I did."

We lifted our bikes and walked side by side across the meadow. A little cool breeze had come up, blowing the tops of the grasses, rustling leaves against our legs.

Annie shivered. "It's strange, isn't it? I mean, Ocean-side's not that big a school and Charlie's the second ...

17

what would you call it? The second . . . *loss* . . . this semester."

I glanced across at her. She was zipping her jacket, not looking at me. "What do you mean?" I asked. "I don't get it."

"I mean Idris. I know it wasn't the same as with Charlie, but still. . . . They were both seniors, and they were both at Oceanside a month ago. Now they're both gone."

I stopped and stared at her. Idris! I'd completely forgotten about Idris.

3

"You're not saying there's any connection between Charlie and Idris?" I asked. "I don't think he even knew her. I mean, Idris was a scuzz." I stopped. "Oops, I shouldn't have said that. You're not supposed to say bad stuff about the missing, even if it's true. Anyway, Idris just ran away to the big city."

"I know. But still."

We were out on the dirt road again, and we got on our bikes.

"You want to go visit Dominique?" Annie called over her shoulder.

"You mean now?"

"Yes. She won't have anybody to talk to about Charlie. I think she'd like us to come by."

"Annie, I've got to try to see Charlie's parents again ... his mom." The thought of still having to face his mother made my stomach heave. "The cops should have gone by now."

"You won't want to stay long anyway," Annie said gently. "I'll wait outside."

But this time there were two strange cars in Charlie's driveway, and I stood there looking at them, telling myself they were family from out of town, probably his aunt and uncle from San Jose. The other license plate was from Salinas.

It wasn't hard to convince myself that I shouldn't intrude, so that I didn't have to see Mrs. Curtis right away. Not that tomorrow would be any better. But it couldn't be worse than today.

"Let's go to Dominique's," I said.

As we rode along I thought about what Annie had said about Idris and Charlie both being gone. But Idris was no mystery. Idris was a doper, the girl friend of DD Hysinger, the head doper himself. The kids said DD stood for dope dealer, dream doctor, dumb doper. There were all kinds of variations on DD's name, depending, I guess on where you were coming from. Idris did anything, and I mean *anything* for stuff, or for the money to buy it from DD. "Even my old lady gets nothing for free," he'd boast.

Idris had been talking for a long time about how she was going to get out of Oceanside, how she was going to split for San Francisco, where there was plenty of action around Market Street and Union Square. One day she left school. Somebody saw her hitching and that was that. She never came back. After a day or two the cops came around, asking questions, then everything died down. I think the kids at O-Hi would have forgotten all about Idris except for her mom.

Her mom is all the time tacking posters with Idris's picture on telephone poles and fences. The past couple of weeks, she's taken to hanging around school, passing out leaflets, asking everyone who walks by if they've heard anything about Idris. If you're lucky and see her in time, you can cross the street before she gets to you. It's simpler that way, because after all, what can you say? "I'm sorry, Mrs. Dellarosa. No, I haven't seen Idris. Not since the day she left school."

Idris's mom is a real sad lady. She looks crazy and she clutches at you and says, "If only I knew where she is. It's easier if you know."

But knowing isn't always that great, either. Charlie's mom knows where he is: Charlie's in the Sunset Mortuary. Is it easier for any of us, knowing that?

Dominique lives on Loma Linda Drive, about five houses from Annie. Loma Linda is definitely the class part of town. You never see regular people when you come round here, just gardeners clipping lawns that don't need to be clipped. I couldn't imagine living here. I can't imagine having a girl friend who lives here, either, and I know Charlie had the same problem.

The gates at the end of Dominique's driveway were open and we saw her house, mellow in the afternoon sun. It looks as if it has been here forever, though actually her father only built it when they moved to Oceanside a year ago. Which shows what you can do when you haul in trees and shrubs that are fully grown and not in one-gallon cans.

This is grape country up here. Dominique's dad came and bought one of the small vineyards outside of town. He put in a manager and he's doing great, bottling under his own label. "Money makes money," as the people round here say, and Mr. Arnaud brought plenty with him and is probably making plenty more. There's no Mrs. Arnaud, though rumor says he's had four wives, presumably one at a time. Now there's just father and daughter.

Dominique's car is a shiny, yellow VW convertible, and today it was parked by the front steps. Annie and I dropped our bikes beside it and went up to the front door. I tried to look as if this is the kind of house I visit every day, but I guess I blew that when I ran my hands across my hair and tucked my shirt neatly into my jeans and bent to try to rub the scuff mark off one of my sneakers.

Annie smiled. Sometimes I wonder how much she knows about me and my inner uncertainties.

The maid who opened the door wore a black dress with a frilly white apron and right off I heard Dominique's voice calling from the cool emptiness of the hallway, "Who is it, Estella?" Then I saw Dominique hanging over the bannister at the top of the stairs.

"Annie! Jed! Am I glad to see you! Come on up."

We met halfway, under a chandelier that would have smashed you flat as a tortilla if it dropped.

Dominique hugged Annie and then stood back and said, "Hi, Jed."

"Hi."

She was wearing one of those soft, velvety tracksuits that might have been pink and might have been blue. Maybe there's a fancier name than tracksuit for an outfit like that. Dominique is very pretty. I don't think she's as beautiful as Charlie thought, but then, it's hard for me to see anyone past Annie. Dom is small, and she has wide eyes that are a purplish color, and her hair is really truly golden.

"She's like one of those little flowers, you know? The ones with faces on their petals," Charlie had said once. His voice had been hushed, as if he were talking about the Virgin Mary.

"You mean geraniums?" I mentioned them because

they're about the only flowers I know. And I only know them because Mrs. Sanchez has a forest of them in flower pots beside her bungalow, which is right across from ours in the court.

"No, bozo, not geraniums! I'll show you sometime."

And he did show me, pointing them out in the mall, asking a woman who was passing what they were.

"Pansies," she'd said, obviously pleased that we cared. "Aren't they beautiful?"

I looked down at Dominique's pansy face now, and I could tell she'd been crying. But there was something else in her dewy purple eyes, something I couldn't put a name to.

She led the way to her room, and Annie and I followed. We sat on a pink satiny couch, and Dominique sat on the edge of her bed. It had a cover the same color.

"How are you, Dom?" Annie asked.

"Awful. I just couldn't go to school. And then I kept wishing I knew what was happening. What did the kids say?"

Annie glanced sideways at me.

"Everybody was real upset," I said. "Most of the talk was about why he did it. Nobody knew."

Dominique nodded. Her foot tapped on the white rug, and she was giving off some kind of vibes. I'm good on vibes. Noah says that's what makes me a great photographer. *Great* is Noah's word, not mine. He says I can pick up on the inside of a subject as well as the outside. But I couldn't pick up on what I was feeling here.

"Did he give you . . . any clue . . . before?" Annie's voice was hesitant. "I don't know what to *say* to you, Dom! Everything seems so heartless. But you know how Jed and I felt about Charlie. Jed *loved* him."

"I know he did." Dominique's fingers traced a circle on the bed cover, and her lashes hid her eyes.

"Had you any idea at all?" I asked. "People who are going to . . . well, you know . . . they're supposed to drop hints. It's like reaching out." I couldn't stand to go on. Charlie? Charlie, did you reach out to me? I didn't know it if you did. Was I doing my thing of keeping just a little distance between us? Did you talk? And did I refuse to listen?

Dominique was saying something, and I made myself listen now. ". . . hadn't seen him for three days. We . . . broke up." Her lashes swept up, and I got a sudden glimpse of those wonderful purple eyes, and the vibes were back. There was something odd here, something that I wasn't understanding. I sat on the edge of the slippery couch.

"Wait a sec," I said. "You broke up? Charlie didn't tell me. I saw him on Friday in class, and he didn't say a thing."

"I guess maybe he didn't want to talk about it. Poor Charlie!" Dominique took a handkerchief from the pocket of her tracksuit and pulled at it, rolling it between her palms. "I said I didn't want to see him anymore, and I've been feeling so awful all day. So guilty."

I knew how she felt, all right. Were we all guilty? Was the guilt like a strand, joining us together? "Did . . . did your father find out?" I asked.

"No. Dad had no idea. This morning he read about Charlie in the paper and he said, 'Dominique? You ever hear of this guy? His name's Curtis, and he went to your school. He hanged himself.' "

"Oh, Dom!" Annie jumped up and sat on the bed beside her, putting her arm around Dominique's shoulders. "How awful!"

They were weeping together, and I stood up and paced

across the thickness of the rug to the window. It was like walking on the back of a polar bear.

"You see, I didn't know when I told him that he'd . . . do this."

Annie made little soothing noises. "Sh! Of course you didn't know."

"When exactly did you tell him?" I asked, and then I said, "Dominique, maybe you think it's none of my business, but I'd really like to hear in detail. I can't stand not knowing — not understanding."

"Sure, Jed. Well, what happened was, he and I were out at McCormack Beach. Charlie had come on his motorcycle, and I was in my car. I keep a blanket in the back. It gets cold . . . you know."

She was watching me, and I said, "I always thought you and Charlie met up on Chitney Trail. Seems like he told me that, or I got that impression."

Her voice quickened. "We did, once or twice. But we haven't been up on Chitney for a long time." Lashes covering the purple eyes, fingers tearing at the handkerchief. "Well, we'd go to McCormack Beach, and we'd spread the blanket in a little hollowed spot by the boathouse where no one could see. It was nice."

Dominique began to pull the zipper of her tracksuit up and down at the neck. The small hiss was the only sound in the room. That and the loud tapping of my heart. Something flickered at the back of my mind and disappeared again.

"And then . . . I don't know what happened," Dominique said. "Charlie got real depressed. Broody. We'd be on the blanket, and I'd say, 'Come on, Charlie! Lighten up!', trying to pull him out of it, you know. But he was really down."

"And you don't know why? You don't have any idea?"

"No." Dominique gazed at me, eyes brimming over, and there was still something there, and suddenly I was doing my camera trick. What I do is, I set the focus for the exposure in my head, and I click the shutter and what I have frozen is an expression. The camera doesn't lie. It takes out your feelings, conscious and subconscious, and what you have left is truth. I had Dominique, frozen in that instant of time and space, and I looked and I knew. Dominique was trying hard to impress me with her sincerity and her caring for Charlie. But there was no caring in my picture.

Maybe she saw something change in my face because she blurted out, too fast, "It got so he wasn't any —" She stopped, then added, "It got so he wasn't the same."

I didn't have the comfort of my real camera to hold so I clenched my hands deep in my pockets. "Were you going to say he wasn't any fun anymore? Any good anymore? So you told him to take a hike? That must have made Charlie feel a whole lot better."

Criminy! Where had all *that* come from? I wondered.

Annie jumped up. "Why don't you take a hike yourself, Jed? Just get out of here."

"You don't understand, Jed," Dominique said. "You —"

I interrupted her. "You're right. I don't understand." I was shaking and I tried to stop myself. "I'll wait for you downstairs, Annie."

I sat in the hallway, out of range of the chandelier if the chain should break. I sat on a polished wooden bench like a church pew, beside a glass table that held a silver tray and a bowl of flowers that was almost as big as the chandelier. Their colors reflected in the glass, and I calmed myself with thoughts about taking a shot of them, using a filter to get a blended effect.

26

The maid came to ask if I'd like to wait in the living room, and I said I was fine, and she asked if I'd like a glass of lemonade. I turned that down too and just sat there, feeling lousy. What right had I to be mad at Dominique? So she'd gotten fed up with Charlie. Annie was right. How could she have known he'd kill himself? Anyway, who was *I* to accuse her of failing him? I don't know much about psychology but this wasn't hard to figure out. If I could blame Dominique, I wouldn't have to blame myself.

I heard a door open upstairs and the soft sound of voices, and then I saw Annie and Dominique at the top of the stairs.

I stood up quickly. "I'm sorry, Dominique. I had no business saying what I did."

Dominique smiled a teary smile. "It's OK, Jed. I'm glad you both came over. It helped to talk."

Annie hugged her. "Call me anytime. Do you think you'll go to school tomorrow?"

"Oh yes. I can't *not* go."

We were on the porch now, and Dominique turned her little, flowerlike face up to me. "Jed? Do you really think Charlie killed himself over me?"

Suddenly I found myself setting my focus again, looking at her. Once, when he'd seen a picture I'd taken of a young pregnant girl and her boyfriend, Noah had said, "Wow, Jed! Is that ever an invasion of privacy! If she *really* saw the way this guy looks at her, she'd do anything before she'd have his kid."

Now I was doing it again, invading Dominique's privacy, hating myself, but doing it anyway. And I saw. Dominique was feeling important. Excited. A guy had killed himself over her. That had to be the ultimate compliment.

I must be wrong though. Dominique had loved Charlie

once. I was sure she had. Even if they'd broken up, there had to be some love left. I clicked another shot of her, and blanked it out before I let myself look at it. I had to be wrong.

4

When Annie's mad at me, she doesn't try to hide it. She took off on her bike and was all the way to her house before I caught up. Even then she'd have gone up the driveway without speaking a word if I hadn't grabbed her arm.

"Hey, Annie! What's the matter? Don't be this way."

"I didn't like how you were with her, Jed. You should have seen your face. You were like the wrath of God. Hasn't she had enough?"

I ran my thumb along her wrist and faked a laugh. "Come on, Annie! You said it turns you on when I'm mean. Besides, I told her I was sorry."

Annie tried to pull her arm away. "Quit it, Jed. Don't you have any feeling for Dom? You weren't the only one who loved Charlie, you know."

"I know." I held on to her, and I have to say I felt pretty uncomfortable keeping her there by force. Annie's house is one of those low, modern jobs with walls of glass. You don't only have to worry about the walls having ears, they might have eyes, too. What if her mother came rushing out and said, "Unhand my daughter, you turkey!"

Once I'd been holding Annie and kissing her, standing by a solid corner, and her little brother, Ethan, tapped against a slit of a window I hadn't even noticed. There's no safe place around Annie's house.

I tried to speak soothingly now. "Hey. Can I come in for a few minutes?"

"No. I'm going to get my swimsuit and go over to school."

"But it's past four."

"The pool will be open. I need to swim."

"I'll ride over with you then and..."

"No." When Annie says no like that, there's no use arguing.

I expected her to head on up her driveway, pushing her bike, her back straight and proud, her silky black hair swinging behind her. And she did take a step or two before she turned. "Jed? Remember, Dominique said it got so it wasn't the same...between her and Charlie?"

"Yes?"

"Well, when we were alone she told me they'd never... gotten together...for the past few weeks."

I could see it was hard for Annie to tell me this. She's real modern, into being a feminist and all that, but she has this little modesty thing that I love. I love it, but it drives me crazy, too, because it stops me from doing things with her I'd like to do.

"Dominique said Charlie...well, he couldn't...." Her face was hidden under the fall of her hair as she turned the bicycle pedal slowly with her foot. I knew her cheeks would be pink, and I realized I was a bit pink myself. Nights, when I'm thinking about Annie, lusting after her, I don't blush at all, no matter how many sexy things we talk about

30

and do in my imagination. I'm always cool and in control. But in real life it's different. I wonder how I would react if I *did* get her in my bed. I took a deep breath.

"I *knew* what she was telling me," I said. "She didn't have to spell it out."

"OK. So that could have been why Charlie..." Annie pushed her hair back, then let it tumble forward again. "I'd better go, Jed."

I took a step toward her and touched her cheek, tracing the curve down into her throat, my mouth suddenly dry from her nearness and maybe a little from what we'd been talking about.

"See you tomorrow, Annie," I said softly, and I watched her till she disappeared round the side of the house, getting the last possible glimpse of her.

Then I cycled home. And I went the long way. Past Charlie's house.

The two cars were still in the driveway, and Charlie's dad was out in front watering the lawn. He was just standing there, with a stream of water coming from the hose, standing in the mud puddle that had spread all round him and was deep enough to cover his shoes. My eyes flashed to the garage and quickly away. The doors were closed but Charlie's red motorbike stood in front of them, gleaming in the sun. It looked obscene; why didn't somebody move it? I made myself ride closer. "Hi, Mr. Curtis."

Mr. Curtis is usually real healthy-looking, probably because he's outside so much. Today his face had that same strange color that Charlie's skin had when he was sick. Gray, like bleached-out wood.

"Hello, Jed." He didn't move the hose. "Go on up to the house."

"Well, I don't know. I don't want to butt in." I stayed on my bike, one foot on the ground, the other one ready to push me off like a rocket blast. God! Mr. Curtis looked awful.

"The house is full of people already. Go on in. Charlie's mother will be glad to see you."

Looking at him, listening to him was scary. A zombie man, I thought — insides all gone. Already I was wishing I'd taken the short way home. Mr. Curtis's back was to me and his head was bent. I could probably sneak away, but that didn't seem right.

I propped my bike on the steps and went to the side door.

It was Charlie's sister, Evelyn, who opened it. Evelyn's in junior high. She's tall and wears glasses, and she's a pretty good basketball player. She didn't say a word when she saw me, just closed the door behind her and came out. We sat down on the side steps.

"You know why he did it, Evelyn?" I asked at last.

"Uh-uh." She'd picked up a little twisted twig, and she batted it against her leg.

We sat some more.

"Who's here?" I asked.

"Aunt Cissie and Uncle George. And my daddy's cousins from Salinas."

I nodded, and we went back to being quiet. I could hear the faint splash of water as Mr. Curtis went on filling his own private reservoir.

"How's your mom?"

Evelyn shrugged. After a minute she said, "I think Charlie tried to tell me." She looked at me, then down again, and I had a quick glimpse of her eyes, swollen behind her glasses. "He came in my room. Last week. He sat on my bed." Her voice was so low I could hardly hear it. "He said everything was hopeless. He said he didn't know what to do next. I thought he was talking about his writing. He'd sent something off to that *Rio Corta Monthly*, the ones who bought his last story. They said they liked it, but they asked him to make some changes and he did. Then they didn't take it after all. That was the day he came in to talk."

She was poking the twig between her tennis shoe and her foot, poking it in and out again. "He wouldn't have hung himself because they didn't take his dumb story, would he?" The twig snapped with a loud pop that made me jump. Evelyn tossed it away.

I shook my head. "Not over a dumb story." My words hung between us, and I remembered thinking that he wouldn't have done it just over Dominique calling it quits or over being temporarily impotent, though that seems bad all right. But not bad enough. Something else had been bad enough. . . .

"I read the letter they sent with the rejection. It wasn't insulting or anything. Charlie was real down, though." Evelyn bent forward so her head and shoulders drooped across her bent-up knees. "You know what I said to him? 'Come off it, Charlie. Everything can't come easy, you know. You should have some real problems, like me. I may not even graduate.' "

Her hands cupped the top of her head as if it hurt. "Sometimes I hated Charlie and I'd wish he'd . . . you know . . . disappear." She shuddered, lifted her head.

"No, you didn't, Evelyn. Not really." I wanted to touch her, but I'm not very good at touching anybody except Annie.

"I *did* mean it. I should have been the one to die, not Charlie. I'm bad. Really bad."

"You're not. Just cut it out, Evelyn." Inside I had a cold, empty feeling.

"Maybe if I'd been nicer that time . . ." Her voice trailed away.

33

"Bull. A guy doesn't kill himself because his sister wasn't nice to him. There'd be corpses scattered all across the country," I said.

"If only I'd told somebody."

We sat in the warm evening sun. A mockingbird called from the telephone wire, and from somewhere in the distance, another one answered. Probably telling each other about the new swimming pool that had just gone in in the Curtis's front yard.

"Do you think I could see it?" I asked at last.

"You mean the letter?"

"It and the story. I don't know what good it will do, but who knows?"

"I'll get them. Or do you want to come in?"

"Not if all the relatives are there. I'll wait." Coward. Cutless coward.

She was back in a minute.

The story was in a brown envelope, one of those big, flat ones that Charlie used for mailing.

"Take it home with you if you like, Jed." Evelyn said. "Maybe I'll send it off somewhere again later. You know, for Charlie."

"Yeah." I touched the ragged brown edge of the envelope, and Evelyn took off her glasses and wiped them on the bottom of her T-shirt. "I'll bring it back tomorrow," I said. "Will you tell your mom that I stopped by and that . . . ?" The words, the ordinary words, wouldn't come out.

"I'll tell her." Evelyn put her glasses back on.

"Do you know yet when the funeral will be?"

"Tomorrow."

"Isn't that kind of soon?"

"I guess not. Tomorrow's Tuesday. He — died — Saturday. It just *seems* soon. Anyway, it's what my parents wanted.

I nodded. "Well, I'll ... see you tomorrow."

Charlie's father didn't look up as I passed. I hoped he'd quit with the water before it started flooding the house.

"Good-bye, Mr. Curtis," I called.

He lifted a tired hand in a tired wave, and I felt a sudden hot stab of resentment at Charlie. Didn't you stop to think what this would do to your dad and mom and Evelyn and me ... even Dominique ... all of us left with a mess of guilt? You're at peace, I guess. But what about us? I couldn't get Mr. Curtis and his puddle out of my head all the way home.

When I wheeled my bike inside our bungalow, it took me a minute to figure out why everything was so bare and neat. Then I remembered this morning, the frenzied cleaning up, the fresh sheets for Annie. Was that only this morning?

I looked down at the brown envelope, and I knew I didn't want to read what was inside. It would bring Charlie too close and I didn't think I could handle that right now. And what if it *did* hold some kind of answer to his death? I wasn't sure I could handle that this minute either. I set the envelope on top of our big TV set that takes up half of our rinky-dink living room and went to check the freezer. It's one of the big chest kind, and *it* takes up half of our rinky-dink kitchen. We could open a frozen dinner stand from what's stored in that freezer.

My father likes the chicken and rice, and the gray roast beef with rubber gravy, and the Swiss steak that looks like something a dog did on the sidewalk. He buys the dinners by the dozen and piles them all in. I stood, staring down at all the unappetizing choices, visualizing my old man

35

sitting hunched over the table, shoveling in, swallowing, shoveling in, swallowing, and me doing the same. Not a word spoken, not a thought exchanged. Years and years of hating me, blaming me. I decided I didn't want to eat right now anyway, and I let the freezer lid slam down. But I didn't want to read that story either.

It was ten after five. I wondered if Annie was still swimming, her long, thin brownness streaking blue through the blue water. Then I remembered that today was the day the photos had to be in for Jim's Camera Shop competition and that he closed at six. My picture was ready to go. Taking it over would be better than staying here thinking . . . or reading.

I got the photo, slid it in a folder with my name and address, grabbed my bike, and was out of there.

Jim looked up when the shop door opened.

"Hey," he said, and sighed the way he always does when he sees me coming. He held out his hand.

"Jim," I began.

"Don't tell me. I know. All it says on our poster is that entries may be submitted only once. No rule against submitting a different one every month." He pulled the picture of the kid wolfing down a banana out of my folder and said, "Hey, this is really good, Jed. Are you still using the thirty-five millimeter SLR?"

"Yeah. The school's."

He slid the photo back in the folder and put it on top of the small pile on the shelf. "Looks like you might win yourself another thirty bucks."

"Here's hoping." I turned, and Jim called after me. "You think you've got a pot of gold here, don't you? Thirty bucks a month, regular as clockwork? Well, one of these days I'm going to change every one of those posters, and you'll find the pot's empty."

36

I grinned back at him. "Bye, Jim."

With any luck I'd have another thirty bucks to add to the money I'd take to Brooks. I had 480 dollars in the bank already, most of them from Jim's competitions. I'd get a job in Santa Barbara as soon as I sized things up. No way was I going to take a penny from dear old dad. If I went to Santa Barbara. Of course I was going to Santa Barbara. Without Charlie? OK, without Charlie.

I didn't feel too bad though as I cycled home, and I knew it had been a relief to talk to somebody who didn't know I'd been Charlie Curtis's best friend. If I'd stayed any longer, Jim would probably have said, "Heard about that kid in your school. Too bad." But I hadn't stayed, and he hadn't said anything, and I knew what a relief it had been to have five minutes when I hadn't thought about Charlie at all.

I'd have to think about him tonight, though. Tonight was reading time.

5

I read the story as I ate my chicken à la king. The king who would voluntarily eat this stuff should have his taste buds examined. I read, and I found nothing.

The story was about the same as Charlie's others, as far as I could tell. It was about a woman going on a train from Lausanne, Switzerland, to Paris, France, and the strange people who got in and out of her carriage. There were long descriptions of her lace jabot, whatever that was, and her perfume and her little silver slippers, which one of the guys who came into her carriage removed so he could kiss her dainty feet.

I made myself read it all the way through twice and I thought about what a terrific imagination Charlie had. Not only had he never in his life met a woman in a lace jabot, but I don't think he had ever ridden in a train. And I know for sure he had never kissed anybody's feet. But everything seemed real and alive, if slow-moving, like the train itself, which one character said was "like a coach to eternity."

Maybe this was supposed to be the story of Charlie's life, and the train station was meant to be his father's garage. But if this was it, I didn't get it. And if there was a reason hidden in the words, a reason for Charlie killing himself, I didn't get that either.

I studied the letter from the editor, visualizing Charlie reading it, feeling so rejected that he went out and hanged himself.

"Bull," I said aloud.

My father doesn't drink, not anything, not ever. So there's never even a beer around. The way I felt I could have used something right then.

I put the envelope back on top of the TV. The garbage was beginning to smell, so I took it out and emptied it into the big, green bin. It was a great night, filled with stars, the scent of some kind of flowers mingling with the stink from the garbage can. Mrs. Sanchez's geraniums glimmered in the dark.

I went inside again, got my box of photographs, and dumped everything on the table.

There were lots of Annie, the camera and I working well together to catch the intelligence in her dark, shining eyes. I had all kinds of candid shots of the kids in school, taken for the yearbook. I stopped at one of DD Hysinger, standing with a cigarette in one hand and a beer can in the other, Idris beside him. Idris, in her too-tight top and too-tight jeans, smiling in that knowing way, one finger pointing at the silver marijuana leaf that hung round her neck. I found one of Lon, sitting on the wall in front of school, a sort of bewildered, innocent look about him. He sat with his feet turned in, toes touching, the way a little kid sometimes sits.

Next door Mr. Yamamoto's TV told me that Western was the only way to fly.

All the pictures of Charlie were in one folder. I slid them out: Charlie laughing; Charlie running; Charlie and Jed at the beach. I'd set the exposure, then rushed to get myself into the shot. My hair was longer then, blonder from days of sun and sea. We'd stuck our surfboards in the sand and stood beside them, the two of us grinning like sharks. Charlie! I sniffed a bit and paced up and down the room, which is not made for pacing, being exactly six steps from one end to the other. I thumped my fist against the wall and then leaned my head against it and cried.

It was after nine when the doorbell rang and I thought, it's Annie. An example of wishful thinking if ever there was one. It was Mrs. Sanchez. Mrs. Sanchez has to be one of the ten skinniest little persons in the world. She told me that, when she was young, someone once posed her in a locker at the bus station and took a picture for the newspaper. "I fitted just fine." She'd still fit.

Mrs. Sanchez looked after me when I had measles and tonsilitis. When I was seven or eight years old I used to sleepwalk. She found me outside a bunch of times and brought me back to bed, tucked me in, and stayed with me. Once, long ago before I was born, Mrs. Sanchez knew my mother.

She stood awkwardly in the doorway now. "Hi, Jed."

"Hi. Come on in." I wiped at my face with the back of my hand.

"Here," she said. "I made tortillas." The brown paper sack she gave me was hot and moist.

"Thanks."

I thought she was going to say something about Charlie and I thought, she doesn't know how to, and I thought, I should help her out. But I didn't know how to either. Please don't say anything, Mrs. Sanchez. I'll start bawling again.

"How's Marina?" I asked.

Marina is Mrs. Sanchez's youngest daughter. She's just started teaching computer science.

"She's fine, Jed. You OK?"

"I guess."

"Do you want to come over to our place? You can sleep on the couch. Or would you rather be alone?"

"I'm OK here. Thanks."

Then she stepped closer and put her arms around me and folded me in her dark, comforting hug.

After Mrs. Sanchez left I put the pictures back in the box, all except the one of Lon. I sat staring at it for a long time. "Maybe he saw her face," he'd said. "Maybe that's why he did it."

"I need to talk to you, Lon," I said. I say things aloud all the time when I'm at home. That could be because I'm alone so much. Or it could be because I'm slightly weird.

I found the phone book in the service porch among the mess of old catalogs and magazines and papers that I'd cleaned up earlier, and I looked up DD Hysinger's number. I don't know Lon's last name, but I do know DD's. Dope Dealer, Dream Dealer Hysinger. There was only one in the book.

A girl answered the phone and when I asked for DD, she yelled, "Dennis! It's for you!"

Dennis?

Her voice sounded young and nice. Probably his sister. It was strange to think that a hairball like DD could have a sister who might be nice and who might be normal.

"Yeah?" he asked. "Who is it?" Wary voice. DD probably has good cause to be wary.

"It's Jed Lennox."

There was a pause, and I knew he was trying to figure out who I was. Then he said, "Sure. The shutterbug."

"That's right. Can you give me Lon's number?"

There was another pause. I could feel suspicion traveling in my direction.

"Lon who?" he asked at last.

"You know Lon who. Your doper friend. The little guy."

"Oh, that Lon. What do you want with him?"

I turned and leaned against the wall. "I just want to talk to him, that's all."

"What about?"

"Nothing much."

"Nothing much, huh? Well then, I guess it's not too important."

He hung up the phone, and I said a word that Annie wouldn't have liked and redialed. The line was busy. I decided the receiver was probably off the hook, and I stood, staring at nothing, trying to think. Why wouldn't DD give me the number? Was he just being a pain, something which was probably real natural for him, or did he not want me to talk to Lon? He wouldn't be able to stop me. But a delay could give him a chance to get to Lon first. He might be talking to him now. "Clam up if that guy Lennox starts asking questions. I don't want you saying anything, hear?" Saying what? "Don't tell him Curtis was mixed up with us." No. Never. Never.

I was looking at Lon's picture again, trying to decide what to do next, when the phone rang and I thought, It's DD. He's decided he might just as well tell me Lon's name. Why not? I've been imagining all sorts of complications here that don't exist. Then I glanced at the clock and saw it was ten o'clock, time for Annie to call. We take turns every night. I fell into Dad's chair, propped my feet against the wall, and picked up the phone. The very thought of speaking to Annie warmed the coldness inside of me.

"Hi," I said softly.

"Jed?" I sat up fast, almost dropping the receiver. It was a terrible voice, dead, toneless. But I recognized Charlie's mother.

"Ah . . . hello, Mrs. Curtis."

"Evelyn said you came over today. I'm sorry I didn't see you."

"That's OK, ma'am." I closed my eyes. Never in my life had I called Mrs. Curtis *ma'am*. This was Charlie's mom. She laughs a lot. She's tall and skinny, like Evelyn, and sometimes she'd come out and shoot baskets with us. I sat on the edge of the chair, knowing something was coming, feeling the knowing in the air, waiting for it to settle.

"Charlie left you a note too," she said. "My sister Cissie just found it. It was folded under the strawberry magnet on the refrigerator door. That's why we didn't see it before." She pronounced each word carefully as if she didn't know the language too well.

Charlie had left me a note under the strawberry? I couldn't seem to take hold of that, even though he always left me notes there. "Jed, I'm going to be late. You go on." "Jed, I'm working on the Brady's yard. Grab a rake and come on over." So he'd left me another note. My hand was slippery on the phone, and I changed the receiver to the other side, wiped my hand on my shirt, put the phone back on the right ear. My voice was having trouble coming out. "Did you . . . read it?"

"Yes."

"What did he say?"

"I'm . . . it's just . . . he told me to tell you last week, but I guess I forgot . . . I didn't know what he . . . I . . ."

"Wait, Mrs. Curtis, I can't understand what you're saying. What did he tell you?"

"How was I to know ... ?"

"Mrs. Curtis," I said quickly. "It's OK. Why don't I come over? Is it too late?"

She didn't answer, but I thought I could hear her ragged breathing.

"I'll be right there," I said and hung up the phone.

6

It was still warm as I rode through the dark streets to Charlie's house. All the shops were locked tight. Even the shoe mender here has bars on his windows. It's hard to know who'd want to steal a bunch of old shoes, but in our neighborhood, you can't be sure. I rode fast, keeping away from the shadowy edges of street and sidewalk, and all the time I was thinking about that note and trying to make sense out of Mrs. Curtis's spacy words. What had Charlie told her to tell me? She'd forgotten, she said. But whatever it was, he'd said it again in the note.

Charlie's house was alight from top to bottom. Only one window was dark, the one above the front porch — Charlie's room, with the drainpipe and the sloping roof that I'd climbed up myself more than once after we'd been out partying. The front yard was a mess of mud, like a dried-up lake bed. I rode through it because there was a bunch of cars blocking the driveway now, left my bike by the steps, and rang the bell. Dead petals fell from the magnolia tree, landing with a soft plop, startling me, surrounding me for a minute with their dry, lemon-pepper smell.

Dave, Charlie's kid brother, opened the door. He wears glasses, like Evelyn, but he's short and built heavy from the waist down. His shape doesn't stop Dave from being an all-star Pony pitcher, though. Behind him I could hear a buzz of voices.

"Hi, Jed," Dave said, and stood aside for me to go in.

It looked like about a million people were in the Curtises' living room, but I guess maybe there were about twenty. My quick, nervous glance told me right away that Mrs. Curtis wasn't there. Mr. Curtis sat on the couch, squashed in with three other people. His eyes were closed, and he didn't open them. I clicked the camera in my head and got a picture of him that was too unbearable for me to look at.

"This is Charlie's friend, Jed," Dave said, and there was a bunch of halfhearted "Hello"s and "How are you doing"s while I stood there, not knowing what to do next.

"Mom went to bed," Dave said. "The doctor left some pills, and my Aunt Cissie made her take them."

I nodded. "What about the note? Did she leave it for me?"

"Yeah." Dave jerked his head toward the kitchen, and I began following him in that direction, weaving through the people. Then I saw Evelyn coming down the stairs. She followed us.

There was a lot of half-eaten food on the kitchen table, dirty dishes, and a big, straw hat with flowers on it. Then I saw the note. It was on top of the toaster on the counter, my name written across the front in Charlie's big, sprawly writing. My heart began to pound.

"There it is," Evelyn said.

I walked across and picked it up and saw the Gemini

46

man, our code, in the right-hand corner. We always put Gemini man, or men, on our messages. Somewhere, back when we were kids, we'd started this, all fired up over the importance of having a secret sign that nobody knew but us. The Gemini men were twins. What we'd do was, if we left the whole message, we'd put two little stick men where a stamp would have been. We hardly ever left a complete message, though. It was more fun that way, and if somebody read the note, somebody snoopy like a little brother or sister, what was written wouldn't make much sense. Not unless you had the other half. An unfinished message had one twin in the corner and a clue inside to the whereabouts of the second half.

I heard someone come into the kitchen now, and I heard a voice ask, "Is your mom sleeping?" and Evelyn answering, "Just about." And then, to me, I guess, "This here's my Aunt Cissie."

I didn't turn around until I'd finished reading Charlie's note, which probably took me about ten seconds from start to finish. It was on a small piece of paper, torn from a telephone pad. "I'll be gone when you get this, Jed. I've left something for you. I'm trusting you to know what to do with it."

I actually read the note twice before I folded it, slipped it in my jeans pocket, and turned to the others.

"This is my Aunt Cissie," Evelyn repeated. "She's the one who found the note."

"Hi," I said. "Thanks."

They were all watching me.

"Do you understand what he meant, Jed?" Evelyn asked.

"We've all read it, you know." Aunt Cissie sounded apologetic.

"That's OK," I said, and I thought, but you haven't read

all of it. You just read what Charlie didn't mind you reading.

"We know what he left you, of course," Aunt Cissie said. The straw hat must have been hers because she lifted it, wiped a smear of mustard off it, and set it on the counter in a safer place.

I guess Evelyn saw my astonished look.

"He left you his motorbike, Jed," she said. "He told Mom you were to have it."

"His *motorbike?*" I stared from one of them to the other.

Aunt Cissie nodded. "It seems he told his mother about a week ago that she was to give it to you when he was gone. She thought he meant, after he left to go to school, and she asked him if the two of you weren't going at the same time."

I licked my lips. "And what did he say?"

"He said he would probably be gone ahead of you and that he wanted you to have it. She thought he meant for you to ride it down there, to Santa Barbara, and she was going to ask why the two of you weren't going on it. But he had some mysterious girl friend and she figured maybe his girl friend was taking him down and that he'd arranged for you to bring the bike. He had a lot of stuff. She didn't pay him much attention. Not till . . ."

Aunt Cissie smoothed out dirty paper napkins on the table, folding them as if getting the edges straight was the most important thing in the world. "It's driving her crazy now, of course. She thinks she should have suspected. He was acting strange. She should have gone to somebody and got help for him. I tell her she couldn't know, but she goes on and on about that. And about how she should have been home Saturday and Sunday instead of coming with Ronald and the other two kids to our place. If she'd been home she thinks she could have stopped him from going out in that garage...."

Somebody's laugh drifted in from the living room. It seemed unholy that anybody would laugh in this house now or ever again.

After a moment Dave said, "I guess Charlie figured I was too young for the bike. And it'll be another year before Evelyn's old enough for a license."

"Yeah." My mind was whirling. The *motorbike!* What did that have to do with Gemini man? Charlie trusted me to know what to do with it. What did he *want* me to do? I rubbed my knuckles across my forehead.

"Would you like a cup of coffee?" Aunt Cissie asked. "I'm going to make a fresh pot."

"No. No thanks. I just came to get the note. I think I'd better go. What — what time is the funeral?"

"Two in the afternoon. At the chapel."

I nodded. "I'll see you there."

"Jed?" Evelyn's voice stopped me. "Please take the bike."

"I will. Sure. I guess Charlie wanted me to but — You don't mean I should take it now?"

"Please, Jed. It just *sits* there. And it's so ... so red...."

Aunt Cissie glanced at her and said quickly, "We *could* put it in the garage. But the garage still has..." She left the sentence unfinished, and I began at once to finish it for her. The garage still has ... the smell of death? The rope hanging from the rafters?

"Can't you just put it in back?" I asked.

"My parents' bedroom windows look out in back," Evelyn said, and I nodded. I remembered.

"I guess I'll take it," I said. "Can I leave my bike?"

"Sure. It'll be OK. I'll bring it inside."

It was Evelyn who got the key and switched on the back house lights. I unlocked the big Honda and stood beside it, unwilling to put my hands on the handlebars or to sit in the seat. I knew why they wanted me to take it out of their sight. This bike was Charlie. Charlie cruising along, his hair bushing out under his helmet — his smile — the gentle dreaminess. "If you go slowly you can see so much, you know? You can tip your head back and see the light patterns through the trees, and the telephone wires are beautiful with the sun moving silver along..."

"Yeah, well don't tip your head back to see all that beauty when *I'm* sitting behind you, bozo!"

Charlie! Charlie! My eyes flickered to the closed doors of the garage. Maybe the Curtises would move. I would. I'd get myself the hell out of here. I touched the damp leather coat of the bike.

"You know how to start it and everything, Jed?"

"Yeah. I'll wheel it out though, in case I wake your mom."

Evelyn came with me to the street. She was barefoot, and she stood rubbing one foot against the other. "Do you think Charlie meant you to do something special with it? I don't get that part about the trusting and all."

"I don't know. Maybe he's just trusting me to enjoy it, to get the most out of life. I don't know. To ride it, maybe, and think of him." I'd think of him all right. Of the days I'd ridden to the beach behind him. Of the times he'd let me take the bike on my own. Of the good times. But this couldn't be what he meant. He'd left it to me for a reason.

"Evelyn," I said. "I don't want to ride this to school tomorrow. I'll walk over in the morning and pick up my bike, OK?"

"Sure, Jed. Whatever. And Jed, if you find out some-

50

thing, some *reason* why Charlie did what he did, will you tell me?"

I nodded.

"Promise. I want to know, whatever it is."

"I promise," I said.

I pushed the Honda about a block and a half before I stopped under a streetlamp and examined it. The seat lifts up on a hinge. I fumbled, not sure how to do it. It took a while, but I got it raised, and saw underneath the small compartment where Charlie kept his registration and a set of tools. I took everything out and laid them on the curb under the yellow lamplight. There was nothing out of the ordinary. I don't know what I'd expected, maybe even a cache of drugs. I studied the registration back and front before I put the stuff back, locked the seat in place, and got back on.

The breeze rushing past my head felt good, the bike powerful and solid under me. I liked the roar of the motor. I liked the speed as I zoomed past the dark, sleeping houses, eating up distance. I pretended that Charlie had lent me the Honda to go see Annie, that he was back there in his room, writing one of his stories or one of those poems that he wrote about Dominique. I was on Hudson now. In a few seconds I'd be home. I couldn't remember, actually, *ever* wanting to be home. Without even knowing I'd done it, I was on Loma Linda, riding past the closed gates of Dominique's house, cutting the motor before I got to Annie's.

I parked the bike and walked under the shadows of the big trees, hoping there were no security cars on patrol tonight protecting Oceanside's richest citizens. In the house next to Annie's, the German shepherd began barking and racing up and down by the gates, but I knew him, and when I whispered, "It's OK, Zola," he clammed up.

Annie's house was all in darkness. I picked up a couple of hard, knobby pods from under one of the trees and padded across the lawn till I was beneath her window. Then I stood back and tossed one of them at the glass.

The window opened at my second try, and Annie leaned out. I put a finger against my lips, and she made a little motion for me to stay right there. In a few seconds she was beside me.

"Jed," she whispered. "What is it?"

"I was over at Charlie's." I told her about the note and the bike and about how awful it had been. But I didn't tell her about Gemini man, because that was Charlie's and my secret, and I couldn't tell that. Not without Charlie's permission. Not even when Charlie was dead. And maybe I wouldn't have told her everything anyway. I don't usually with anyone.

"Poor Jed." She stepped closer and put her head against my chest, her arms circling me loosely, and as soon as I felt her against me, everything else disappeared. She was wearing one of those short nightgowns, white with blue flowers on it, and when I pulled her closer, my hands were on the warm, smooth skin of her back. I could smell the sweet, night smell of her. The Annie smell.

"Oh, Annie!" I was groaning into the midnight shine of her hair. "Come back with me, Annie. There's nobody there. I don't want to be by myself, not tonight." I heard myself and I was ashamed, because everything I said was true, but I knew, in a way, I was using the situation. Using Charlie's dying and Annie being sorry for me.

"Jed, sweetie." She sounded ready to cry. "I can't. You know I can't. Look, come inside. I'll fix coffee. We can sit in the kitchen. You could even sleep on the couch if you want to. It'll be all right. Mother will understand."

52

"Why does everyone think I want coffee and to sleep on a crummy couch? That's not what I want, Annie. I want you."

"I know. And I want you. But I'm not going back with you, Jed."

I took her face in my hands, running my thumbs along her cheeks. "Then put on some clothes. Come for a ride with me. Please. Just a little way."

She looked at me for the longest time, and I thought for sure she was going to say no.

"Wait here," she whispered and was gone as quickly and as quietly as she'd come.

When she came back she was wearing jeans and her old red, white, and blue Olympic sweat shirt. Her hair was tied back with a red scarf.

We went hand in hand across the grass, and I kept thinking of all those watchful windows in the house behind, waiting for a shout or maybe the clang of an alarm bell. But there was only the loud chirping of the crickets and the sleepy voice of a night bird.

Zola whimpered to come with us, his nose pressed against the fence, but Annie whispered, "Some other time. Be a good dog now," and he quit.

She gave a little whimper herself when she saw Charlie's bike.

"I know," I said.

I watched her touch the seat, just the way I'd touched it, and I knew she was remembering, the way I'd remembered. When I got on, Annie climbed behind me, her arms tight around my waist, her body tight against my back.

I gunned the motor and headed for Chitney Trail. At the meadow we slowed and bumped gently across the tufted grass. Then we got off and stood, looking down across the Edge of the World. Far away to the left was the on-again, off-again flash of the beacon at Peyton Point. The sea was a pewter band that striped the far end of the dark chasm below. If we could lean out, we'd have seen the twinkling lights of Montecito. But up here we were alone.

I took a deep breath. The air held that faint eucalyptus smell, like the rub Mrs. Sanchez used to put on my chest when I was little and had a cough. I wondered if Charlie had stood here, breathing in the smells of Chitney Trail, stood with his arms around Dominique. As if she'd picked the thought from the air between us, Annie said, "I wonder why they stopped coming here. It's so beautiful and so private. So much nicer than McCormack Beach."

"I don't know why they stopped." I was thinking of Dominique telling us how they'd spread the blanket in the little hollow, and how they'd lain on it, and I felt heat building inside of me. I turned Annie gently to face me and we were kissing. Her lips opened and her hand was behind my head, pulling me closer, our breaths mingling, her heat mine, mine hers.

My hands were under the sweat shirt, moving upward along the delicate ridge of spine, the feelings overflowing inside of me the way they always do when I touch her. Her breath was as fast as mine, and I eased her away a little and slid my hands around in front, cupping the smooth roundness of her breasts. Our faces were almost touching. I saw her dark eyes close. I heard her moan.

And then she moved, one slow, sure move that took her away from me. "Jed," she whispered, "it isn't that I don't want you. But I'm not ready. And you're not either."

"What do you mean I'm not . . . ?" I began, feeling the readiness about to explode inside of me.

She put her finger against my lips. "You've got things the wrong way around, Jed. You want to be physically a part of me, as if that will start us off on something wonderful together. I don't believe — I don't think that's the way it works. I *don't*, Jed. It's kind of — I think it's the sharing that comes first. Sharing important things, like the way we feel and what makes us hurt. Stuff like that. I'm willing to give that to you right now. To me, that's the real commitment. But something's stopping you. I'm not sure what."

She traced the outline of my face, my eyebrows, my jaw. "When we have that, then the other . . . the making love . . . that'll be the seal. Don't you see?"

"Oh, come on, Annie." I smoothed back a strand of her hair. "We're not talking about which comes first, the chicken or the egg. We should do what we feel like. But I want whatever you want." I was lying though. I wanted more, and I wanted it now.

She touched my lips again, then kissed me gently before she turned toward the darkness.

I stood behind her, the top of her head tucked under my chin. I tried not to think of the way her breasts had felt, and I tried not to let my mind linger on how they would look. Paler than the rest of her. Softer.

"The stars are so bright," she whispered, and I took a deep breath to cool the heat inside of me and looked up at the sky.

There it was, the Gemini constellation. I pointed over her shoulder. "See that cluster with the two really bright stars? Those are Castor and Pollux . . . Gemini . . . the Heavenly Twins. They're always together."

Except now. One was missing from Charlie's note, hidden somewhere, waiting for me to find it.

7

After I took Annie home I rode some more, zooming through the night, and the stars, to McCormack Beach, finding a little hollow by the boathouse that might have been Charlie and Dominique's place and might not. I got off the bike and sat on a sandy hummock and listened to the waves sighing against the shore.

For a minute I let my mind linger on me and Annie. For me, sharing everything is the real commitment, she'd said.

I wasn't going to be good at doing that. There'd been too much silence in my life, too much time spent keeping my guilts and broodings to myself. The closest I'd ever been with anyone was with Charlie and that had taken a lot of years, a lot of forwards and backs. And I guess in the end I hadn't known him that well, either.

So OK, concentrate on Charlie now. He'd killed himself. Maybe Dominique had some idea why. Maybe Lon, the doper, did too. But I knew I was grasping at straws. What could they know? Then there was Charlie's note. He wanted me to do something. Avenge him? How could you avenge someone who'd killed himself? By finding who or what had driven him to do what he'd done and taking care of them. And to do that I had to find the other Gemini man. I pulled out tufts of the coarse grass and let the wet sand clot through my fingers. Somebody had hurt, humiliated, bugged Charlie so much that he'd walked out that night to his garage and cut off his air supply forever.

I looked at the dark bulk of the bike that I'd left up on the gravel road. Then I stood, brushed the sand off me, and headed for home.

I still keep my house key on a string around my neck. I guess old habits die hard, and I've had that key hanging there for as long as I can remember. There's an extra one hidden under the bottom step, but I've never needed it. I opened the door wide then went round to the vacant lot where Dad keeps his camper when he's not off in it somewhere. There's an old plank back there. I got it, propped it against the steps and began pushing the Honda up. The bike's not light, and I was groaning and shoving, and the steps were sagging, and I found myself wishing Charlie was at the back pushing too to make it easier. What a crazy thought!

The door of the bungalow next door squeaked open and Mr. Yamamoto came out on his top step. I gave a final shove and got the Honda up on the level surface, half in and half out of the door, and then nodded in Mr. Yamamoto's direction.

"Ah, Mr. Lennox," he said, and bowed politely. I've told him a bunch of times to call me Jed, but since he's only lived next door to us for eight years, I figure he doesn't think he knows me well enough.

Behind him I could hear the yammer of his TV set. He

was wearing light pajamas with knee-length bottoms, but I don't think he'd been asleep. Mr. Yamamoto never sleeps. Round here he's as good as a watchdog, except that he doesn't bark. He doesn't talk much either. Tonight he surprised me.

"Your friend's bike," he said, smiling. "Your friend who came."

I nodded. Mr. Yamamoto doesn't take the *Sentinel* so I figured he didn't know Charlie was dead, and I didn't feel like explaining.

"My friend who came," I repeated. Mr. Yamamoto smiled some more and disappeared.

I stood the Honda under the hanging, central light in our living room. The room was so small and the bike was so big there was hardly any space left to step around it. The wheels had left a dirt track across our stained rug, but who'd care? Not me. Not Dad. Not our crummy landlord, who hasn't set foot in the place in my lifetime.

I drank a glass of milk from the refrigerator and got to work.

There wasn't one half-inch of that bike that I didn't examine, checking under the seat again, prying off the rubber handgrips to feel around inside the hollow tubing of the handlebars. No place that a note could be taped or wedged escaped me. I even got a flashlight and unscrewed the gas cap to look inside the tank. I took off the headlamp. I removed the yellow California license plate and checked behind it. Then I stood back and did my imaginary photograph trick, using the Nikon F with the twenty-eight-millimeter lens that's Noah's pride and joy, turning the bike picture I'd snapped upside down and sideways.

That bike was clean. I sat in Dad's chair and nibbled my nails.

"What the hell were you talking about, Charlie? Where

is Gemini man? Why did you have to be so damn subtle?" It was 3:30 A.M., and I was tired and frustrated.

I had another glass of milk and buttered two of Mrs. Sanchez's tortillas, wolfing them down. Then I hit the sack to the sounds of Mr. Yamamoto's TV telling me about the joys of Oscar Mayer bologna. Just as I was drifting off to sleep I thought, maybe I should just quit all this. Charlie was dead. So what if I did find out why? That wasn't going to bring him back. But I wakened in the morning knowing that I'd failed Charlie when he was alive. There was no way that I was going to fail him again, now that he was dead.

Then I remembered that today was Tuesday, the day he would be buried, and I groaned and turned my face to the wall. I remembered too that my old man probably didn't know about Charlie. Not that he'd worry about it that much. He'd met Charlie a couple of times, though, so I figured I should tell him.

I called the Callahan Construction Office, and they put me through to the building site. I told the foreman to ask Dad to call me.

After I hung up, I said out loud, "OK, Charlie. I'll start by talking to Lon. I'll find out what he meant about that face. I'll find out *whose* face and if he knows something, he'll tell me or I'll wring his scrawny little neck."

I'd set my alarm a half hour early so I could walk over to Charlie's house and get my bike. It was up on the Curtises' porch, chained to one of the wooden porch pillars, so I had to ring the doorbell. It was Dave who came and unlocked it for me. I was glad it was Dave and not Mr. Curtis or Charlie's mom.

Since I'd told Annie I wouldn't be meeting her, I went straight to school.

Glenn Ponderelli and Bob Rothman were standing outside under the big fig tree, collecting money in an old coffee can. Taped to the can was a scrap of paper that said "Flowers for Charlie Curtis." I emptied my pockets. There wasn't much there except my lunch money, but I gave it all. The can was half-full.

"How's it going, Jed?" Glenn asked, not quite meeting my eyes.

"OK, I guess."

"You going to make it to the funeral?"

I didn't look at him either. "Yeah, I'm going to make it to the funeral."

The day was as awful as I'd known it would be. Everywhere I looked there were memories of Charlie. The basketball hoop where we used to play. His locker. Somebody had cleared it out and the door swung half-open. He'd had a poem of Robert Frost's taped inside, the one with "miles to go before I sleep." I pulled the door wider. The tape was still there, hanging by its corners, but I guess the poem went with the rest of his stuff, to his parents, or wherever.

Annie was waiting for me in front of English class, and she took my hand, gave it a squeeze, and half led me to my desk. She put her mouth close to my ear and whispered "I love you" before she went on to her own place. I turned the words over and over in my mind the way you'd turn a magic pebble in your hands. Annie loves me. Loves me. Loves me.

At lunchtime we saw the announcement about Charlie's funeral on the notice board. It would be at 2 P.M. today. Anyone who wanted to attend would be excused from afternoon classes. I stood looking at the printed words, trying to make myself realize that this was the day they would put Charlie into the ground.

"Dominique's here," Annie said. "I saw her earlier." She

pushed her hair back and gave me a nervous look. "Do you think we should . . . you know . . . ask her to sit with us at lunch?"

"Go ahead, Annie. You eat with her. I'm not being unfriendly again, but I've got something to do. Anyway, I'm not hungry."

I had no lunch money either, but I didn't mention that and it wouldn't have mattered. Annie has bought lunch for me more than once.

"Is what you have to do — about Charlie's note?" Annie asked.

"Sort of."

She nodded. "OK, Jed. I guess you don't want to tell me any more. So we'll meet right after fifth period and walk to the church. You *are* going to fifth period?"

"Might as well. No point in arriving early for a funeral."

Annie's dark eyes searched my face and then she said sadly, "You make things so hard on yourself, Jed. Didn't anybody ever explain to you that a trouble shared is a trouble halved?"

Dominique was coming in our direction, and I didn't answer. Instead I ran my hand along the smoothness of Annie's arm and said quickly, "Thanks for coming with me last night. It helped. I'll see you later."

As soon as she left, I headed across the street to the park, which is where the dopers hang out at lunchtime.

A couple of the kids lined up by the snack truck spoke to me as I passed, and I could feel that mixture of awe and embarrassment because they knew I was Charlie's best friend. What does he know that we don't? they were wondering. Not a whole hell of a lot, I thought.

The dopers were in their usual place, clustered around one of the beat-up wooden tables in the far corner of the park. Most of them had their backs to the outside world, which is their normal attitude. I looked for Lon, but I couldn't see him. I did see DD though, and his trusty sidekick, Monk.

When I was a few yards from them they turned in my direction. I smelled the musky, sickening sweet smell of marijuana mingling with tobacco smoke. A few opened bottles of Coca-Cola stood on the table, the Coke probably used to wash down God knows what.

I still didn't see Lon. I looked around at the circle of watchful faces and felt a sinking hopelessness. Charlie! Charlie! You didn't get yourself mixed up with this bunch, did you? Tell me no, Charlie.

"It's the shutterbug," DD said. "What do you want?"

"I'm still trying to find your friend Lon," I said.

DD's fingers played with the silver marijuana leaf that hung from its chain at his neck. I guess they all wore one of those, like a fraternity pin. The Brotherhood of the Weed.

"You're out of luck. Lon didn't make it to school today."

"I need to know where he lives then," I said.

"What does he want him for?" somebody asked, the voice surly, and there was a sort of growly murmuring all around. It made my scalp tingle. No way did I want to mess with this doped-up lot.

DD held up his hand. "Why don't you do us all a favor, yourself included, and forget about Lon?"

"I'm not going to forget about him."

"Want to take his picture, do you?" somebody asked, and tittered. "Little Lon's so — cute."

"I don't think that's what he wants," DD said.

I kept my eyeballs riveted on DD's. "I want to ask him about 'her face.' "

" 'Her face'? Whose face?"

62

Was there a shifting, a small tightening of his jaw muscles? Was there an odd hush around me or just an ordinary, listening silence?

"The girl's face," I said softly. "The one Lon saw. The one Charlie Curtis may have seen too."

"The guy's freaked," Monk said. "You must have got ahold of some good stuff." His voice was cool but I sensed his watchfulness.

"No. No stuff." I grabbed the arm of the kid standing next to me. He looked younger than the rest of them. He might even be Lon's age. "Quick," I said. "Win the grand prize. What's Lon's last name?"

The kid's mouth opened, but no words came out. He looked at DD.

"Sammy doesn't know Lon's last name," DD said.

I let go of the skinny arm. "This is dumb. All I have to do is go down to the office. Or find one of the girls in Lon's grade and ask her, or . . ."

"So do that, Shutterbug." DD twirled his silver marijuana leaf. "No sense us making it easier for you."

I went straight off to the office, but there was only a student on duty, and she said Miss Bellingham, the secretary, had gone for lunch and wouldn't be back till one. "And then she'll be going off again to the funeral — you know, the guy who died."

I nodded. "I'm trying to find a kid called Lon something. He's in ninth grade. Could you let me have a look through the list of ninth grade students?"

She stared at me blankly.

"You know . . ." I urged. "There has to be a list of all the kids registered for ninth grade."

"I'm not sure where it's at. If there is one. And anyway, I couldn't let you see it. I have no authority."

I came around the back of the counter, and she edged

away as if she thought I was going to attack her. "You can't come back here. This is just for office personnel."

I was pulling out a green file drawer. "You see, I'm the school photographer," I said, "and I took a picture of this guy, Lon, and I can't put a caption on it if I don't have his last name. . . ."

The hanging files in the drawer were alphabetized, but since I didn't know Lon's name that wasn't much help.

"I'll call Mr. Haig," the girl squeaked. Mr. Haig is our big, mean old janitor. "You'd better get out of here."

And then, fortunately for her and unfortunately for me, the door opened and Mrs. Carruthers, the principal, came in.

"What's going on here?" she asked.

I slid the drawer closed. "I was just trying to find the name of one of the boys I photographed," I said, and I backed toward the right side of the counter with my hands up in front of me as if to ward off her blows. "It's OK. I'm going."

"I tried to stop him," the girl wailed.

I said, "It's true. She did. But I'm in kind of a hurry. The yearbook . . ." I let my explanation trail away.

I saw Mrs. Carruthers considering the situation, and I saw that look come on her face, the one that said she had remembered I was Charlie Curtis's best friend. Then I saw the softening. "Don't pull something like this again, Jed. If you need information, go through regular channels. We'll help you."

I was almost home free.

"Who is this boy you're looking for?"

"That's the trouble. He's in ninth grade. I don't know. He's new this year. First name's Lon."

She thought for a moment. "Well, of course all the ninth

graders are new this year. Why don't you bring in the picture you took? One of us will be happy to tell you. That is, if you can't ask Lon himself."

"He wasn't in school today," I explained, by now right at the door, ready to make my getaway.

"So bring the picture tomorrow," Mrs. Carruthers said.

"Yeah. OK. Thanks."

I stood outside in the hallway. Maybe Lon would be at Charlie's funeral. This funeral was going to be the ultimate worst. But I was beginning to have bad feelings that time was passing — that the trail, if there was a trail, would get colder and that I shouldn't let that happen. Not when Charlie had trusted me.

The Robert Frost poem slid into my head. I was the one who had some promises to keep.

8

It looked as if all of O-Hi was jammed into the little Chapel of the Saints of Heaven. It was too warm inside, and the air smelled of too many flowers. Glen and Bob had taken their coffee-can money and bought four great bunches of white and red and pink flowers with long stems. They stood by the church steps and gave each of us one as we went through the doors.

"Carnations," Annie said.

Before we even sat down, I saw that coffin up in front with the pile of wreaths on it. Mr. and Mrs. Curtis and Evelyn and Dave were in the front row beside Aunt Cissie in her straw hat. Probably the backs of the heads in the seats around them belonged to the relatives from last night. I saw Mrs. Carruthers, the principal, with a bunch of teachers from school, Miss Bellingham from the office, and Noah, sitting by himself a few rows in front of Annie and me, his bushy black hair, his bushy black beard. He turned around when I came in and gave me a nod and a solemn look. Big Eddie and Eddie Jr. from the 7-Eleven were right beside us. They must have closed up shop. I'd never seen that shop closed a day in my life. And then Idris's mother came walking up the center aisle.

She was wearing a long black dress with a frill at the neck, and her streaky gray hair hung down her back like a mane. The rubber beach walkers she wore were black, too, and I saw healed scratches and fresh bite marks on her feet. Under her arm was a bunch of leaflets.

"Oh, no," Annie whispered.

Idris's mother walked up that aisle like a bride going to her groom, and everyone began whispering. I got an anxious feeling in my stomach. But two men in dark suits, from the church, I guess, got up and steered her gently into one of the rows, and she sat down without any fuss and bowed her head.

Annie had been saving the seat beside her. I hadn't asked who she was saving it for, and when Dominique slipped in next to us I wasn't surprised. Dominique twirled one of the pink carnations, and I noticed that it exactly matched the pink shirt and skirt she wore. Instantly I flashed on to her, standing outside the church, choosing, getting her colors perfectly coordinated. Sometimes I wonder where my rotten thoughts come from.

She leaned across Annie and gave me a teary smile.

The Saints didn't seem to have ministers, just ordinary guys the same as the ones in the dark suits. Probably they were all like Charlie's dad, working at regular jobs and "doing a little preaching for the Lord on the side."

One of them stood and said a prayer that was mostly asking for comfort for the family and friends of "our brother in Christ who has departed from us," and then he sat down and another stood up and led us in singing "Abide with Me." There was no organ. I didn't know the words and I could tell Annie didn't either, but still, there was enough good sound in the little church to choke us up. And all the time I was looking at that shiny brown coffin, visualizing Charlie inside. Not the way he must have been when they cut him down, but the way I knew him. Charlie, lying in there with that dreamy look on his face, that wide, gentle smile.

And then I was almost undone because Evelyn went to the front and said she wanted to say a few words about her brother. She was terrific, calm and strong, and saying true, strong things about Charlie that hurt so much I could hardly stand it. Annie was sniffling. So was I. So was everybody in the church. I didn't look at Dominique.

Afterwards, we all straggled behind while Charlie's dad, Dave, and two of his uncles carried out the coffin and walked with it the two blocks to the cemetery.

But the worst thing of all was that squared-off, waiting hole in the ground. They stood the coffin on a trestle thing beside it and I tried not to look down inside the hole as we all filed up with our carnations, and I looked at the pile of flowers instead of into that gaping, scary space. Everything was a blur, the colors slashed with the diamond brightness of my tears.

When I came back to my place, Eddie Jr. was there.

"Is it OK for me to give this to Charlie?" he asked in a loud whisper. He stroked the big, red shiny apple he held. "I always gave Charlie the best apple when he came into the store. I liked Charlie."

"I know you did," I whispered back. "It'll be OK."

"My dad said it would be OK."

"It is OK. Go on up."

Eddie set the apple right in the middle of all the flowers

on top of the coffin, and none of the men in the dark suits said a word. Then Mrs. Curtis stepped forward and hugged Eddie, and Charlie's dad shook his hand.

There was another hymn, this one about amazing grace, and then it was over. We drifted out of the cemetery, leaving Charlie behind in his shiny brown box. I thought it was a very good idea not to put it into the hole till we'd all gone.

I moved around a little, checking the crowd. Lon wasn't there. None of the dopers were. Right now, feeling the way I felt, if I'd seen one of them, he'd have told me Lon's name, his address, the color of his eyes, his height and weight, and what he ate for breakfast in two seconds flat, or else.

Mrs. Sanchez was standing at the side, under one of the tall, skinny cemetery trees. I hadn't seen her before but she came over to us and grabbed my hands and said, "Jed. I took a couple of hours off to say good-bye to Charlie."

"That was nice," I said, and I thought what a sweetheart Mrs. Sanchez was. She works in a beauty shop, shampooing hair, and if she takes time off she loses money as well as the tips she gets from "her ladies." The shop's called Harvard and Mrs. Sanchez has some pretty good jokes about how she's been "four years at Harvard." She says pretty soon she'll be ready to graduate.

She squeezed Annie's hands too and smiled politely at Dominique. "I have to get back, Jed."

"Thanks for coming."

And then Evelyn came over and touched my arm.

"My parents want to know if you'd like to come back to the house. It will be just family and a few close friends." She gave Annie and Dominique apologetic looks. "My mother's not up to having too many people."

"How could she be?" Annie asked, and Dominique gazed off somewhere past Evelyn's head. I doubt if Evelyn even knew who she was. For sure, she didn't know that Dominique had been closer to Charlie than any of us. Well, for a little while anyway.

"Jed?" Evelyn asked.

"I..."

"You don't have to. We just thought you should be asked." Evelyn pushed back her glasses and blinked at me. "I'd like to skip it myself if I could. It hurts too much."

I nodded, trying to get some words out. "Tell your mother..." I swallowed.

"I'll tell her. But I think she knows." Evelyn was walking away when she turned. "Oh, you're to stop by and get Charlie's helmet. My mother says you're not to even get on that bike without it."

"OK. I'll remember."

"What bike was she talking about?" Dom asked as soon as Evelyn left.

"Charlie's. I don't want to get into this now, Dom. He left me the Honda. That and a note."

"A note?" This time I wasn't imagining the quick nervousness in Dominique's voice. "What did he say?"

"He wants me to do something for him."

"What? How can you do something for him? He's dead."

"Oh, he's dead all right." I walked between them, my mind in a whirl.

Idris's mother stood by the cemetery gates, looking like the angel of death in her long black dress.

"Oh, no. There's that crazy old woman," Dominique's voice was low and shaky. "Wouldn't you think she'd have enough... enough manners not to be passing out leaflets about her daughter *here*? Now?"

Mrs. Dellarosa was indeed passing out leaflets, pressing them into people's hands as they passed, whispering hurried little words.

"Poor thing," Annie said. "I expect this is hard for her. She probably wakes up every day of her life wondering if Idris is alive or dead."

"Let's not stop, whatever we do," Dominique muttered.

I glanced down at her. This was a nervousness that went way past embarrassment over Mrs. Dellarosa's lack of manners. The vibes I'd had about Dominique yesterday were crawling all over me again. I slowed as we got close to the gates, hoping some of my thoughts or suspicions, or whatever they were, would take better shape. I'd keep a close watch on Dom from here on in.

But Dominique moved quickly, slipping past Idris's mother and through the gates on the far side of a cluster of kids, leaving Annie and me behind.

Annie looked around in bewilderment. "What happened to Dom?"

"She took off," I said. "She probably needed to be by herself. Probably felt too heartbroken to hang around."

"Why do you have to be so *mean* about her all the time?" Annie asked.

I shrugged. "I honestly don't know."

9

Some of the kids stayed for a while after the black car with Charlie's family moved away from the cemetery.

"I think I'd like to go to the pool now," Annie said in a low voice. "Go to the pool and swim and swim and swim in that nice clean water." She slumped a little and closed her eyes. "Want to come, Jed?"

"No. I'm going to go down to the lab. Noah probably went back already. I'd like to work till I can't think anymore. But I want to hang around here for a while first."

Annie's glance flickered past me. Over my shoulder, she could still see Charlie's coffin, the mound of earth. "You shouldn't *be* here, Jed. It won't do any good."

"It's OK. There's someone I want to talk to."

"I can see you're not about to tell me who."

"Yes, I am. Idris's mother. I didn't mean to make it sound like a secret."

"But why? Why do you want to talk to her?"

"I'm not sure. I'm looking all the time now, Annie. And I don't even know what I'm looking for."

Annie's eyes softened. "Well, don't stay around this place any longer than you have to."

"I won't," I said, and squeezed her hand.

As soon as she left, I walked back to where Mrs. Dellarosa still stood by the cemetery gates.

She looked up when I spoke her name. "You've had no word at all about Idris?" I asked.

"No." She pushed her long hair back in a gesture that was hopeless, but still so like Annie's that it startled me. "The police aren't doing much. There are too many runaways." When she tilted her face toward me, I saw that she had little pockmarks on her skin. "It's hard for me to make them believe Idris isn't any runaway," she said.

Her voice had been getting louder and louder and I spoke softly, trying to soothe her, "But isn't that the most likely ... ?"

She interrupted. "I *know* she didn't run away. I know because of the meatloaf."

I tried to look sympathetic, but I was beginning to think she was slightly spacy, and no wonder. Spacy people make regular people nervous. That could have been all that was bothering Dominique.

"Idris doesn't like the way I make meatloaf, so *she* always does it," Mrs. Dellarosa said. "Why would she take a package of ground round out of the freezer in the morning if she wasn't planning on coming home?"

"Maybe she planned on you making hamburgers?"

"No, no!" Mrs. Dellarosa stamped her foot as if to say "Here's another one who won't listen." Idris smiled wistfully up at me from the pink flyer.

"She'd left out a package of frozen sausage, too. Idris uses both in her meatloaf." Mrs. Dellarosa paused. "I told the police all of that, but they didn't pay any attention."

The meatloaf mystery, I thought. I didn't blame them

for not listening. Not when everybody in Oceanside probably had told them how Idris was all the time talking about hitching to San Francisco. Besides, hadn't Mrs. Dellarosa considered that Idris might have just decided to go on the spur of the moment?

"Something *happened* to her," Mrs. Dellarosa said.

I felt so sorry for her standing there. Mothers had it hard a lot of the time. This one. Charlie's mom. Mine. I didn't want to think about mine.

"I hope it was nothing bad, then," I said, and I added, "with all the things you have to worry about, it was nice of you to come today."

She half smiled, nodded. "I wanted to come. Charlie was a good boy. *He* came to see me."

"Charlie? Charlie came to see you?" I heard my voice as loud as hers had been, and I tried to bring it down. "You mean, before he died?"

"No. Just after Idris . . . vanished." Mrs. Dellarosa's eyes looked beyond me, into a place too painful for me to follow. "I was sitting in the dark, in my kitchen. He came. He rang my doorbell. He wouldn't come in. He told me he was sorry."

I couldn't get a grip on this. "Sorry about what?"

"Sorry that she'd gone, of course. He said he knew how bad it must be for me."

"I didn't think Charlie — Did Charlie even *know* Idris?"

"Oh, yes. They went to the same school."

Which didn't mean a thing, of course. I stood there, stunned. Why would Charlie have gone to this woman's house? Just because he was nice, kind, sensitive? I couldn't see it. But if he *had* known Idris he'd kept quiet about it. Maybe Dominique knew. Maybe she thought he had good reason to be nervous. "Did he say anything else?"

74

"No." Mrs. Dellarosa was bobbing her head up and down now, her shoulders moving slightly as though keeping time to some beat inside her head. "Such a nice boy. He didn't cry. But he was close to it. I could tell. He felt for me." She stopped moving for a moment. "I asked a lot of people why he killed himself like that. Nobody would answer me. Do you know?"

"I wish I did. I'm trying to find out."

"Did it have anything to do with Idris?"

"With Idris? I don't think so."

"He felt bad about her disappearing. I know that. But to kill himself..." She was bobbing again in that strange way, and I was thinking, She can't really believe Charlie would kill himself because of Idris! And then I was thinking, But I don't know for sure. Nothing makes any sense.

"I offered to play the organ for the funeral," she said, "but they don't have music."

Vaguely I remembered that Mrs. Dellarosa used to teach piano out of her house. She put her hand on my arm and I saw that the nails were bitten down into the flesh, and then she bent close and whispered, "I'll tell you a secret. Her real name was Iris. She didn't think that was different enough, so she called herself Idris. She was the prettiest baby. Baby Iris. It's a flower, you know."

"It's a nice name," I mumbled. "Sure. Iris. That's nice." I edged away a couple of steps. "I hope she comes home soon, Mrs. Dellarosa. Good luck."

Baby Iris. I felt rotten. I'd thought of Idris as a scuzz ball, and a doper, and worse. But to her mother she was Baby Iris and she was gone. I looked back and Idris's mother was still standing there by the gates, motionless as a crow in her long black dress, and I thought, what a great picture: the cemetery behind her, the sky and the thin, dark trees. I focused, framed it perfectly, the shadows on the grass, a pale finger of sunlight touching a marble angel on a grave marker. Fantastic. I could see the caption. "Mourning Time." And then I thought, it's not *her* son lying behind in that coffin, and I thought, anyway, how can I be taking an imaginary picture like this, a picture of her, suffering? I must be really, truly rotten all right.

And in my head was another picture, an incomprehensible one, of Charlie, tears in his eyes, standing in front of Mrs. Dellarosa telling her he was sorry.

"He felt bad about Idris disappearing," she'd said. " 'But to kill himself . . .' "

10

Usually, as soon as I go into the lab I feel better. I love the smells and sounds. The walls close around me like a cocoon, like a womb. But today the comfort didn't come.

I was working on a color posterization, using different sets of negative-positives, printing them on colored papers.

Noah came behind me and tapped me on the shoulder. "Hi, Jed. Will you stop in the office when you're through? I want to give you something."

"Sure."

I tried to concentrate on what I was doing, but my thoughts got in the way. That coffin . . . Charlie's mom and dad . . . Mrs. Dellarosa. After about a half hour I gave up, took my poster into the dark room, and fed it into the processor. It takes fifteen minutes to dry, so I left it there while I went to see Noah.

It's always a mess in his office, but a nice mess. Stacks of old photo magazines clutter desk and floor. The walls are covered with ads for visual art exhibits or prints by Bruce Archie and people like that.

"Jed!" Noah began rummaging through the long top drawer in his desk as soon as I came in. "I've got this somewhere. Sit down."

There wasn't anywhere to sit, not unless I cleared a bunch of stuff from his only scrappy chair, so I stood, examining a poster on the wall above his desk. It was a shot of a straight glass jar filled with a bunch of droopy-looking flowers.

When I leaned closer, Noah glanced up.

"Are those irises?" I asked.

"Irises?" Noah's teeth gleamed white through his beard. "No, you bozo. Those are tulips. Irises are usually white or dark blue, sometimes purple or yellow."

"Like pansies," I said. "I'm really getting to know flowers. Carnations today."

"Yes," Noah said softly. "Carnations today." He found a small scrap of paper that he handed to me. "Here. This guy's at William Cooper High in Agee. He's going to be starting at Brooks in the fall too, and he needs a place to live in Santa Barbara."

The name Rick Pastori and a phone number were scrawled in pencil.

"I told him I might know somebody with a place who needed a roommate," Noah said.

I stood, looking at the unfamiliar name.

Charlie and I'd zoomed down to Santa Barbara on his bike. We'd bought a paper, and we'd sat at a little table in a patio place, drinking coffee and circling ads for rooms that looked possible. Pigeons had walked, splay-footed, on the dull red tiles by our feet. A guy at the table next to us played a harmonica.

I'd thought that living with Charlie would be strange. It would take some getting used to, like having a brother, like

78

having a father. I'd laughed out loud, picturing Charlie in a father's role.

And now, this stranger. This Rick Pastori.

Calling him would be an end to something. It would be a letting go of Charlie. I wasn't ready yet.

"I'll have to think about it," I said.

"Sure. He's a nice guy." Noah pressed the junk in the drawer flat so he could jam it shut again. "Don't wait too long, Jed. That wouldn't be a good idea."

Our eyes met, and it was the way it always is with Noah. The words were on different levels. He'd said one thing, but he meant more.

"I'll decide soon," I said.

"Jedediah!" Sometimes Noah calls me that because he says it's a pity to waste a great name like mine that's straight out of the good book. "You don't look so terrific, kiddo. Take a day off. Get yourself away from here."

I stuffed the paper with Rick Pastori's number in my top pocket.

"There's a Shirley Burden exhibit down in Mendocino. Why don't you take your girl this weekend and go check it out?"

"I might do that," I said "Thanks, Noah."

I rode to the pool on the way home, but there was just a lifesaving class practicing artificial resuscitation on the deck. Annie had gone. I was halfway along Hudson before I remembered that I hadn't taken my poster out of the processing machine. No sweat. Somebody would do it for me.

I got off my bike outside our bungalow and was fishing my key up from under my shirt when Mr. Yamamoto's door opened.

"Hi," I said.

Mr. Yamamoto's TV was blasting, the way it always does, and he was bowing and smiling the way he always does. But today he'd added something. He was pointing toward the step, then toward our door. "The key," he said. "I gave it to her. She was waiting."

In eight years I had never heard Mr. Yamamoto make such a long speech. I looked from him, to the step, to the door. "She? There's somebody inside?"

"Very pretty girl." I'd never seen Mr. Yamamoto smile a real smile before either. Usually he just gives me one of those polite jobs. "OK?" he asked.

"OK," I said. "You can always give the key to a very pretty girl."

He pointed to the steps again. "I put it back. Good there for emergencies or waiting friends." The word *emergencies* gave us both a lot of trouble. Mr. Yamamoto to say it, and me to understand it. He bowed himself back inside, and I thought, My God, Annie's here. She's changed her mind about the chicken and the egg.

I did a quick, frantic inventory of how I'd left the place. I remembered the almost clean sheets and immediately I got quivery inside. I smoothed my hair, stood, not knowing whether to knock on my own door or use my key. But I didn't have to do either. The door was opened from inside, and Dominique stood smiling at me.

"Surprise," she said. "I hope you don't mind. I wanted to talk to you, and the nice man next door let me in."

"Dominique!" I could have wrung her neck for not being Annie, but I made do with a scowl. "Excuse me," I said, and I wheeled the bike past her and parked it in the living room next to Charlie's Honda.

"Do you always bring everything inside?" Dominique asked, and I nodded. "I wouldn't have it long around here if I didn't."

80

Dominique smiled. "It's a good thing you don't have a horse."

It wasn't much of a joke, but it made me mad anyway. What made her think she could joke right after Charlie's funeral?

She was staring round our little box of a living room and she said, "You know this is really quite nice. It would be cute if you fixed it up. Flowered wallpaper, Tiffany lamps."

"You want to move in?" I asked. Oh, Annie would be *so* mad if she could hear how surly I was.

Dominique giggled. "Not really." Her toe poked at our bald rug. "I wouldn't be surprised if there's nice wood under here."

"I wouldn't be surprised if there's termites." I took off my book bag and hung it on the doorknob and I thought, Cut it out, Jed. You don't have to be this hostile. *She* didn't make Charlie kill himself. It's not that simple, and you know it. So maybe she contributed. So maybe we all contributed. So just cool it. But there's something about her that I don't like and don't trust. OK. Try to remember that Charlie loved her.

She perched on the arm of Dad's chair. "It's just you and your dad, isn't it? Your mom died when you were born. Charlie told me." Her voice was suddenly soft. "I guess neither of you two men is into decor."

"Not much." I wondered what else Charlie had told her. That my father had never stopped blaming me? I'd come too soon. I'd done everything wrong before I even took my first breath. That I'd killed her. "I didn't see your car," I said.

Dominique swung her leg. "I left it farther up the street and walked back."

"Well, I hope you still have hubcaps. And tires." I glanced at her quickly and away. She was still wearing the pink skirt and shirt. Her legs were bare and smooth and brown, and I could see quite a lot of them. The skirt had buttons all the way up the front, and the three buttons on the bottom were unfastened. I tried to think if they'd been that way before, but I couldn't remember. I did remember the matching carnation.

"Where's your flower?" I asked.

"My flower? Oh, I left it in the car. It was a nice funeral."

"Sure. If you're into funerals." I went past her to the refrigerator. "Would you like something to drink, Dominique?"

"Oh, yes, please. Something sugar-free, if you have it."

"How about water? That's sugar-free."

"Oh Jed!" I heard her little laugh. "Water's fine."

I tipped the ice cubes into the sink, then washed them off under the faucet, as our sink is not the world's most hygienic place.

I stood to drink while Dominique sat, one long brown leg swinging, violet eyes smiling at me over the rim of her glass. "Good."

"Comes free with our rent," I said. "That and the garbage pickup." I was looking directly at Charlie's bike, and I was thinking that he'd known Idris and that something had happened to her. Suppose he'd hit her, when he was out riding on the Honda? Suppose he'd left her lying... hit and run. No! Charlie would never have done a thing like that. Never in a million years.

I set my empty glass carefully on the table and crouched in front of the bike, examining the shiny red paint on the front fender, the gleaming chrome spiked wheels. Not a scratch.

"What are you searching for?" Dominique asked.

I stood, ashamed at myself for even looking. "Nothing,"

I said. "But I'm glad you're here, Dominique. I wanted to talk to you."

"About Charlie?"

"Well sure. What else? Did he ever mention Idris Dellarosa to you?"

"No." The word came too fast. Her gaze was too direct. I knew she was lying.

"Oh wait." She swirled the ice in her glass. "He might have said something about her running off. I mean, everybody was talking. But that's all."

"Never said he knew where she'd gone or anything like that?"

"Of course not. Why would Charlie know?" She paused. "You never told me what was in the note he left." Her leg stopped swinging. The ice lay quiet in the glass.

"I did tell you. Charlie asked me to do something for him."

"Yes. But you didn't say what."

"Do you want some more water?"

She shook her head.

"A frozen spaghetti dinner? Frozen haddock and chips?"

She shook her head again and gave me a piteous smile.

When I came back from the kitchen, I saw that she hadn't moved but that there were now four buttons open on her skirt. Maybe those buttons were loose and came free by themselves. But I didn't think so. I thought, Dominique's coming on to me. So what if it's because she wants me to tell her exactly what was in that note? So what if opening these skirt buttons had helped her before to find out things she wanted to know? Whatever her reasons, coming on to me was lousy. My throat closed with a mixture of rage and humiliation for Charlie.

"Jed? Will you promise to tell me before you do . . .

whatever Charlie wanted you to do?" She looked at me with misty, purple eyes. "We need to be sure it's right for him. He's dead. We don't want anything that would make ... anybody think less of him."

She lowered her head. "While I was waiting for you I kept looking at Charlie's bike and ... I keep wishing I'd been ... you know, more *patient* with him. I'm a really loving person, Jed. I need to express the way I feel about a guy to the ultimate. I couldn't stand it when it was less, for Charlie and me."

She straightened, and her eyes met mine. "I know some girls aren't this way." She probably knew, or guessed, about me and Annie. How *I* wanted to, and Annie didn't. And she'd better shut up quick. But Dominique had more to say.

"I'm too honest, Jed. I can't tease. I have to give everything."

Next door Mr. Yamamoto's toilet flushed with a sound loud as Niagara Falls, and I wanted to laugh. Perfect sound effects.

Dominique stood up. "I have nobody to talk to about it now, you see. If I could just talk to *you*, Jed."

"You could talk to Annie anytime."

"Well, Annie's nice, and she tries to understand. But she can't. You and I are the only two who really felt this way about Charlie."

I stood with my hand on the seat of the Honda. "If you want to talk about Charlie, go ahead. I'm happy to listen."

Her face got a little pink. "I couldn't start in, just like that. But maybe we could take a drive to somewhere quiet and ..."

I shifted my hands to the Honda's handlebars. "Should I come separately ... on this?"

Dominique's color deepened. "Jed! You don't have to be so ugly to me. Charlie would have wanted us to help each other —"

I interrupted. "*Let's* help each other, then, Dom. I'll give you, word for word, what Charlie said in that note if you give me whatever it is you know. You *do* know something, Dominique. And it's about Idris."

"No, Jed. No."

I grabbed both her arms above the elbow. "There's a tie-in somewhere. Was Charlie sleeping with Idris? Paying her?"

Dominique gasped and tried to pull her arms from my grasp. "How can you say such a thing? Charlie loved *me*."

"Well, what then? Was he buying dope from her? Selling it?"

Someone knocked on the door. "Yeah? Who is it?" I let go of Dominique's arms.

"Maria Sanchez. Can I come in?"

"Sure. It's open."

Mrs. Sanchez had a folded newspaper in her hand, and she stood just inside the living room looking from me to Dominique and back. "Excuse me, please, Jed. I not know you had company."

"It's OK. This is Dominique. This is my friend, Mrs. Sanchez."

Mrs. Sanchez nodded politely and then held the paper toward me. "You no see this, Jed?"

"The *Sentinel*? Uh-uh. I went to the lab after school and I just got in."

"I buy it on the way from work." Mrs. Sanchez was hovering, uncertain, looking again at Dominique.

I was beginning to have a creepy feeling that I'd been through all this before. Wordlessly, Mrs. Sanchez held the

85

paper out and I took it, remembering instantly yesterday morning ... the 7-Eleven, holding the *Sentinel* just like this. "It's not something new about Charlie?"

"No. Not about Charlie. You read, Jed."

I unfolded the paper.

Smiling up at me was a picture of Lon. He was wearing a shirt and tie and a shy smile. He looked younger. Underneath it said JAMES DELAWARE LONNIGAN FOUND DEAD.

"You know him, Jed?" Mrs. Sanchez asked. She stood there, ready to comfort me again, to shield me from more pain.

"No," I said. "Not really. I didn't even know his name."

11

I know I walked Dominique to her car because I wouldn't let any girl wander alone on our streets when it was almost dark. I remember saying to her, "You mean you didn't even lock it? You have to be crazy. I'm surprised you still have a steering wheel."

I remember her whispering in a stunned kind of way, "Oh, that poor kid. Poor Lon. It's all so awful." She put her hand on my arm before she got in the car and looked up at me and said, "Jed, don't forget, you promised to let me know if you find . . ."

I opened the door for her. "Dominique, I didn't promise anything."

I know I called DD Hysinger.

"His name was James Delaware Lonnigan," I said, without even telling DD who was speaking.

"I guess so." DD was using the same, wary voice.

"The paper said it was accidental death," I said after a pause. "They suspect a drug overdose. They'll know more after the autopsy."

"Yeah, yeah. I read the same paper you did."

"What do you think, DD? *Was* it accidental?"

"Could have been. Who knows?"

"I don't think so. I think it was because he saw 'her face.' "

I'm not sure which one of us hung up the phone first, but I do know it was after a long, pulsing silence.

My old man called later, and he was grumpy as hell.

"I tried to get you three times today. Where've you been? Don't leave me a message like that if you're not going to be around. I even tried the Sanchezes'. There was nobody there either."

I sat on the arm of the chair where Dominique had sat earlier. The stale bungalow air still held a trace of her perfume, some kind of flower. Essence of pansies. My father can't stand Mrs. Sanchez, and she's not exactly crazy about him, either. When they meet they're like two cats with their backs up.

"You give this boy a neurosis with your crazy talk," she'd say. "He no kill his mother. *You* know that."

"Mind your own business," he'd shout back.

The first time I heard Mrs. Sanchez say that I'd thought *neurosis* was another word for the sleepwalking I used to do. Then I looked the meaning up in the school dictionary. "A functional nervous disorder." After I looked up *functional*, I decided that Mrs. Sanchez was right, except that I probably had a neurosis already.

Now I said, "Both the Sanchezes work, and I go to school. You've probably forgotten. Then I went to a funeral."

"Who died?" Dad asked.

"Charlie Curtis."

I don't know what I expected him to say. Something rotten.

"A smashup on his bike?" Dad asked at last, and there could have been sympathy in his voice. I wound the phone cord around my wrist and tugged on it.

"No. He hanged himself in his garage."

"My God!"

I clung to the phone, listening to the silence. "Well, I know you liked him," he said at last. "It's bloody hell when somebody you care about dies."

The words could have been his way of saying he was sorry. Or they could have been a reminder to me of what I'd done seventeen years ago. With Dad you never know. I unwound the cord from my wrist.

"Another kid from O-Hi died today too."

"Another kid hung himself?"

"No. He OD'd."

"A dopehead. No loss!" One thing about Dad. He stays pretty true to form. "There'll be fireworks when the news-people get hold of this," he said. "Two kids from the same school in the same week."

"It's been in the *Sentinel* already."

Dad gave his little bark of a laugh. "The *Sentinel*? I'm talking about the bigger papers. Maybe the *Chronicle*."

"Yeah. Well."

We'd run out of conversation, but at that we'd talked more than we usually do. "How long are you going to be gone?" I asked, thinking it would be OK with me if he said a couple of years.

"Five, six weeks."

"OK."

We were finished. I hung up, and I remembered how Charlie used to always finish his conversations with his parents with a quick, muttered "Love you." That would have been nice. If I ever did it, though, Dad would faint dead away. And if I ever did it, it would be a lie. I wondered if he was right about the newspapers.

He didn't seem to be. The only press guy around school next day was Morris Mohrman from the *Sentinel*, nosing about to see if anybody knew anything.

"You got any recent pictures I can use of the kid?" he asked me. "He's only ten years old in the one we've got."

Morrie and I've done business before. I had the shot of Lon sitting on the school wall, but I wasn't about to give him that. One photograph by me of one dead guy in the *Sentinel* was enough. "Why don't you check with his family?" I asked.

Morrie stuck his pencil behind his ear, the way newspaper men do in the old movies. "The kid lived with his mother and his two sisters. I tried. They won't open their doors. The only thing we know is, he's being cremated. We're working now on getting a picture from whatever school he went to last."

Morrie flipped over the pages of his notebook. "I got a quote here from a psychologist who specializes in teens killing themselves. 'One suicide gives permission for another to follow.' I'm going to use that. That Lonnigan death was another suicide all right. I guess the kid thought Curtis gave him permission."

"Hey," I said. "Don't try to lay this one on Charlie." But I felt instinctively there was a tie-up between the two deaths. Life is full of coincidences all right, but this wasn't going to turn out to be one of them. Lon had linked them together for me himself.

"My old man thinks this is going to hit the big-time press," I said. "Two kids in the same week from the same school."

"You saying the *Sentinel's* not big time?" Morrie showed

90

his funny little teeth in a grin. I don't know if those teeth are his own or if he had them made, but God or somebody goofed on size. "Anyway, your old man's wrong. It would take more than two deaths to make a splash. If there's a third . . . or a fourth . . ." He wiggled his eyebrows.

"You're sick, you know it?" I asked.

"You never hear of multiple suicides?" Morrie called after me. "You never hear of that town in Texas where they had seven — all in the same year?"

I kept walking. Seven suicides in the same year! Two were pretty small potatoes then. I heard what I'd just thought, and I said out loud, "God, I'm just as sick as Morrie is."

At that time, though, I didn't know what I found out the next day. Two *can* be enough . . . if one of them is the son of a U.S. congressman. And if that congressman is a member of the President's Commission on Drug Abuse.

"Lon's father is who?" Annie asked, aghast.

We were sitting across the park from school under one of the big, gnarly old trees. There wasn't much of lunchtime left. I'd cycled home fast to check out the mail because I'd got the idea in my head that maybe Charlie had dropped the Gemini man note in a mailbox and that I'd get it today. Which made no sense, because he'd have had to mail it at the latest on Saturday, and this was Wednesday. But I was beginning to grasp at anything.

"I caught about thirty seconds of the San Francisco news when I was at the house. Lon was James Delaware Lonnigan III. His dad divides his time between Washington, D.C., and some town in the Midwest. The parents are divorced."

Annie shivered. "His poor mother. Why do things like this happen to people who already have too much to handle?"

91

"They probably don't. It just seems that way."

Annie covered her eyes with her hands. "What's happening here, Jed? First Charlie, now Lon..."

"And don't forget Idris," I said. "Where's Idris?" I lay back and looked up at the sky through the shimmering green leaves, and Annie leaned across me and tickled my face with a piece of grass.

"Poor little Lon," I said. "I wish I *had* found him and talked to..."

Annie interrupted. "Jed, there's a woman and two men heading right for us. One of the guys has a bunch of camera stuff."

I sat up. For a minute everything was blurred after the brightness of sky, and then my eyes focused and I saw the three of them. The woman was out in front. She wore a tight skirt and heels, and she was having trouble in the rough grass. The two guys were young. The one lugging the camera was black with a mustache and the beginnings of a beard. It was the other one, the one with the mike, who spoke to us.

"Which of you two is Jed Lennox?" he asked, and smiled a Hollywood kind of smile to show us he was cracking a joke.

"I am." I felt stupid already because I'd answered his stupid question so seriously.

"We're from Channel 3 News," he said. " 'What Happened Today Tonight.' *We search for the truth.*"

"I've heard it," I said.

He raised an eyebrow. "You mean, you've seen it. We're TV, fella, not radio."

"I know. I hear you just about every night." Coming over loud and clear from Mr. Yamamoto's, but I wasn't about to explain.

"Oh. Well, we were told we'd find you two over here. I guess this must be Annie ... ?"

He glanced quickly at the woman, and she supplied Annie's last name. "You're Jed's girl friend, huh, Annie?"

"Yes." Annie got up on her knees and moved a little closer to me.

"Hi, Annie. I'm Bob Whistler, the ugly guy with the camera's Gene Thomas, and the lady with all the class is Ellie Peck."

The lady with all the class smiled and took off her wraparound sunglasses.

"Jed," Bob Whistler said, "we understand you were Charlie Curtis's best friend. That he was closer to you than just about anybody — outside his family. We were thinking he probably had a girl friend, and you and Annie and he and ..."

"No," I said.

"Hm." His sharp eyes considered me, and the woman scrawled something on her notepad. "Well, we wondered if you have anything to say to our viewers about Charlie and James Delaware Lonnigan. Was there, maybe, a connection?" He loaded that one word *connection* so heavily that I knew exactly what he was insinuating.

"If you mean, was Charlie, who was black, supplying James Delaware Lonnigan, who was white, with illegal substances, no. There may be a drug connection in this school, but Charlie Curtis was no part of it." I tried to keep total eye contact, to not waver or blink.

"You understand that there's a lot of interest in young Lonnigan's death. His father's up there, you know ... important?" Whistler's quirky smile invited me to share in how ridiculous it all was that the viewers would be interested in a kid just because he was the son of a congressman. But that's why they were here. Charlie's suicide wouldn't have rated this much attention.

"Charlie Curtis's father is pretty important too, you know," Annie said. "So was Charlie."

I scrambled to my feet and pulled her after me, and I saw Bob Whistler give her that old up-and-down, eyes-lingering-here-and-there look. Annie stared at him, and he got suddenly very interested in his microphone, tapping on it, making adjustments.

"Why don't you go find somebody else to talk to?" I asked.

"Oh, we have. And we will some more. Don't you worry. We'll find out whatever there is to find out." Whistler didn't like us. It was in his voice and in the tight line of his lips. We hadn't been cooperative. Probably TV people are used to cooperation.

The photographer nodded to me as we passed. His eyes met mine, and I saw a glimmer of sympathy. Another time I'd have liked to stop, take a look at his camera, and talk about what he did for a living. But not now. I was all of a sudden jumpy and jittery. What if they did find whatever there was to find about Charlie and Lon? What if it was something horrible?

12

Thursday morning, when I was bumping my bike down the steps of the bungalow, Mr. Yamamoto appeared on his front step. He shifted from one foot to the other, pushed his glasses up, ran his fingers through his spiky hair.

"You see TV?" he asked.

"This morning?" I shook my head, and he shook his along with me.

"Last night."

"Yes." And suddenly I knew why he was looking so uncertain. "You saw that awful 'What Happened Today Tonight' show, didn't you?"

Mr. Yamamoto's shoulders moved up and down, helplessly. "Not that. Regular news. Little bit. I not know before. I see your friend. Your friend who came."

I nodded. "Yes."

"He good boy." Mr. Yamamoto nodded with his own words. "I very sorry."

"Thanks."

He bowed politely and began backing inside.

I thought how nice people could be, ordinary people like Mrs. Sanchez and Mr. Yamamoto. He'd been listening for me next door, not wanting to intrude, waiting till I came out so he could tell me he was sorry. I got on my bike, and my chest was aching so much I could hardly breathe. I wondered how long it would be before I'd stop aching every time Charlie's name came up. Maybe never.

We were swamped with TV and newspaper people that day. They weren't inside school, but they were all over the place outside. Everybody was getting into the act, talking to them, hamming it up for the cameras. It seemed every kid at O-Hi had known Lon real well, had been his best buddy, had sat next to him in class, had walked with him to school, had had him over to listen to records. Which was pretty weird since Lon had never hung around with anybody as far as I could see except the dopers. And the dopers stayed away from the camera.

I saw Ellie Peck and the other two from "What Happened Today Tonight." They were talking to Eddie Jr., and he was smiling all over his not quite right face and lapping up the attention. Probably nobody had listened to him so intently in all of his life. I wondered if they were bugging Charlie's parents too, tramping through the dried mud to the front door, making the Curtises suffer all over again.

They'd been there all right.

That night, eating my Icelandic cod and watery mixed vegetables with the side order of apple sauce, I watched it all on TV. Charlie's house, Lon's house. The picture of Charlie that I'd taken and that had been in the *Sentinel*. God! Lon's bedroom window . . . the "room where he'd been found lying on the floor beside the bed." O-Hi and bunches of kids I knew telling how shocked and surprised everybody had been at what had happened.

I sat up straight. There was the park, and Annie and I, looking somehow belligerent, looking like the kind of teenagers you wouldn't want to be around, and me asking "Why don't you find somebody else to talk to?"

I tossed my empty foil plate in the direction of the garbage bag but missed. A rectangular plate with compartments doesn't fly well, especially if there's still a hunk of Icelandic cod weighing it down. Round plates have better velocity.

They were showing the Hill now, in Washington, D.C., and a quick, hurried shot of Congressman Lonnigan getting into his limousine. The Commission on Drug Abuse got another mention.

I'd bought a bag of chocolate-chip cookies, and I began eating my way through them. There was Idris's mother, holding a picture of her daughter for the cameras, talking earnestly about the meatloaf. Asking anyone who'd seen Idris to get in touch. And Ellie Peck was saying "So tonight the town of Oceanside is in turmoil. What is happening, the good citizens ask each other? Two of their children, dead by their own hands. One vanished into thin air. Should we be doing more? Trying harder to understand?"

"Yes," I said. "Go talk to my old man."

Ellie Peck leaned toward the camera. "And Idris Dellarosa . . . if you're watching tonight, you know how worried your mother is. Get in touch, please. Tonight she is carrying a heavy burden. Only you can set her mind at rest."

My stomach was doing those funny things again. It might have been the Icelandic cod but I didn't think so. It was the Idris syndrome. Somehow, for some reason, the thought of Idris could do this to me. I stood up fast and switched channels and there was Eddie Jr. saying, "Charlie Curtis was my friend. I miss him. He always talked to me. He always bought an apple in our store. I always gave him the biggest one."

"Why did you do that, Eddie?"

"Because I liked Charlie. He was my friend. I don't know what made him . . ."

I couldn't bear it anymore, and I switched it off. But I could still hear Eddie Jr.'s voice droning on and on, and I cradled my head in my hands and covered my ears. It was no good, though. The sound was coming through the wall from Mr. Yamamoto's apartment next door.

13

On Saturday, Annie and I were riding through the morning, through the cool white sun and the cool, tangy smells on the coast road to Mendocino. I felt her in back of me on the bike, felt the heat of her, her arms wrapped tightly around me.

Far below the sea glittered blue and green, shadowed with the darker, dancing shadows of kelp. Oceanside was behind us. So was the week with all its pain. It was wise of Noah to suggest that we leave today, and wiser still for him to give me a reason to leave. Today I wouldn't think about death.

We stopped at one of the turnoffs that give a view over the ocean, and I shut off the motor. Birds hopped in and out of the dry brush on the cliff below us. One, blue as the sea itself, and with a long, forked tail, defended its territory with a noisy cree-crr-cree.

We got off for a few minutes to unwind, then rode again, and in another half hour we were in Mendocino.

We'd both been there before, but for me it was different,

seeing it with Annie. Mendocino is constantly changing now that the tourists have found it. But it's still real, not fake and pretentious like Carmel.

The old hotel on the front had a new look, like some ancient lady all decked out in a new wardrobe. I could still see her elegant old bones and fine porcelain skin, though.

"Let's go in and have coffee," I said, and Annie looked aghast.

"Jed! They probably charge five dollars a cup in there."

"Naw. They wouldn't dare. Besides, I'm rich. Jim called last night. I'm thirty bucks to the good. My banana boy won the photography prize."

Annie grinned. "Again? I bet they hate you, all those poor slobs who aren't as good."

"They can have the contest to themselves after September." The remembrance that I'd be in Santa Barbara without Charlie sobered me up, and I tried to remember the name of the guy Noah had suggested who might want to share a room, but I couldn't. I couldn't remember where I'd put the scrap of paper with his phone number, either.

We sat on wicker chairs at a table by the window in the lounge. Across the street was a swath of grassy scrub and beyond that the ocean. Tourists walked by our window, glancing in at us as we drank our thick, rich cappuccino.

The Burden exhibit didn't open till one, so when we finished our coffee we got our towels from the bike carrier and walked a narrow sandy path between shrubs and wild flowers to the beach. Little kids played in the shallows while their mothers sat under umbrellas. A dog was the only swimmer. His black, sleek head slid over the waves and we could hear his excited, gulpy barks.

We stripped off our clothes that were over our swimsuits and rushed into the water. I couldn't believe it was so cold,

cold enough to take my breath away. Annie plunged through a wave and came up, her head as dark and shining as the little dog's, making wuffly puppy noises too.

We splashed around, tossing handfuls of the sparkling ocean at one another, diving for legs, coming up close enough for cold, wet kisses. And then it was the way it is for us sometimes, the laughter dying, the questioning wanting looks, the holding each other, the frantic straining to get closer.

There is something about standing waist-high in the ocean, the waves thrusting against you, the sun warm on your shoulders, holding the girl you're crazy about, that's like nothing on earth. I slid my hands across the smooth wetness of her stomach, round to the back, down to the tops of her thighs just below her bikini and I said, "Can you believe that I'm standing here, freezing to death, and I need to take a cold shower quick?" I tried to laugh, but that laugh died too and we were kissing again, her lips parting, and I'd never known such a needing.

"I think I love you," I whispered against the warmth of her shoulder. "There's no other explanation."

"Me too. Oh, Jed, you won't forget me when you go to Santa Barbara and meet all those beautiful models ... ?"

"Sh." I touched her lips with my fingers. "Never."

It was too cold to keep our swimsuits on when we came out of the water so we found a corner by the cliff where driftwood and fallen logs made a natural barrier, and we stopped and toweled off, Annie behind one pile, I behind another.

I'd offered to share my space. I'd offered to help her in any way I could: dry off her back, hook her bra.

"Not wearing one," she said. "You can't wear a bra and a bikini top, fellow."

"No bra?" I'd pretended to faint. "You're driving me crazy!"

I'd offered to dry her feet for her, and I'd thought about kissing them, the way the guy had done in the train in Charlie's story. I'd suggested she might like someone to hold on to for balance while she got into her jeans.

She'd grinned and said, "One day I'm going to take you up on one of your lewd suggestions and watch you run scared."

"How about today?" I asked quickly, and she shoved me and ran, and I slipped in the sand and had to go into that cold ocean again to rinse off. Oceanside seemed a million miles away.

Afterwards, as we walked back along the beach I saw a dead gull at the waterline. The little black dog was sniffing around it and so were a few dozen sandflies. I turned my face away. No death today. Please, no death today.

I spent a lot of time at the exhibit, engrossed by the incredible detail and the intense composition of Burden's work. I took notes, and I made rough sketches. I wondered if I'd ever be this good and decided that I would. With Annie beside me, I could believe anything.

Later, we bought cheese and fruit and ate on a hummock facing the ocean, and then we browsed through the Mendocino shops. Mostly they sell antiques. I don't know how genuine the antiques are, but the buildings are old all right, and they have plaques on the outside to prove it. "Built in 1830," things like that. I touched the wooden lintels by a door and wondered who'd lived there in 1834, what their dreams had been, and if their dreams had come true.

In a gift shop, Annie saw a silk kite that was shaped like a hawk in flight. "Isn't it gorgeous?" she breathed. "And so real."

The owner began immediately to pull the kite down. "I'm only looking, really," Annie protested. "Please don't go to all that trouble."

"It's no trouble at all." The woman held the hawk by the fragile wood strips on its back, lifting it so it hovered above our heads. It was big, bigger in her hand than it had seemed before, and I remembered once being out at McCormack Beach with Charlie, seeing a hawk rise from the bluff to hang between the clouds.

> *I am the hawk in the windswept sky*
> *Watching the world go hurrying by,*

Charlie had said softly. Sometimes when he said things like that, I didn't know if he was remembering or making up lines as he went along.

I am the hawk, I thought now, and I reached out my hand to stroke the one the woman held.

She smiled. "It was made in China. Once I saw an old man flying a kite exactly like this in the People's Square in Beijing. I tried to take his picture, but he saw me and turned his back. The old ones over there don't like to be photographed. They believe that each time you take a picture, you drain away a little piece of the soul."

"It may be true," I said, and Annie gave me a disbelieving look.

The hawk watched us with its proud, fierce eyes.

"How much is it?" I asked.

The woman showed me the tag: $24.00. "It was thirty-six dollars, but it's been hanging up there for a year now." She stroked the silk. "See the beautiful workmanship? And this is all balsa wood construction in back, so light."

"We'll take him," I said.

103

Annie turned to face me. "Jed! You need your money. You can't . . ."

I was fishing for my wallet. "Sh, Annie. I don't want to leave him here."

The woman smiled from one of us to the other. I guess all the world loves a lover, and for sure every salesperson loves a spender.

"How will we get him home?" Annie asked softly.

"He'll fly behind us, how else?"

The saleswoman took my twenty and ten and gave me change. "It snaps apart in back and folds. I'll show you. And there's a box." She gave me an amused glance. "Of course, if you're determined to fly him, he does come with this nice wooden spool of string. Do you know, the old man in the People's Square had a spool that was exactly the same? Isn't it a small world?" She gazed at us, bright-eyed. "Where are you two nice young people from?"

"Oceanside," I said, and I saw the knowledge come and her smile disappear.

"Oceanside! Oh, my, it's terrible what's been happening up there. Those young lives. Did you know either of the two boys?"

"Yes," I said, and whatever was in my voice stopped her from asking more.

No death today, lady. Please, no death today.

We all three stood in silence as she took out the wood in the back of the hawk and rolled the kite till it lay in a silken tube on the counter. One hawk eye still watched me as she fitted the roll into its box. I saw Chinese characters printed black on the blue cardboard.

"You'll be able to put it together again with no trouble," the woman said, a little flurried by the impact her questions had had. She put the lid on the box, shutting the

104

hawk away from the light, and I remembered that other box, that shiny, wooden coffin box.

"We'll take him the way he is," I said quickly. "No box."

"Of course."

When we got outside, I gave the rolled-up silken hawk to Annie. "Will you keep him for me?"

"You bought him for a special reason, didn't you?" she asked softly. "And maybe for a special time, too."

"I don't know."

"I think it has to do with Charlie."

"Yes," I said. "It has to do with Charlie."

14

While Annie and I were swimming in the ocean, buying the kite, sharing our magical day together, something dreadful happened. And that night, or rather in the early hours of Sunday morning, while I slept to the chatter of Mr. Yamamoto's TV, something else was going on.

I woke up late, toasted some bread I found in the freezer, and ate it with peanut butter for breakfast. Then I pulled on shorts and a T-shirt and cycled to the 7-Eleven for a Sunday *Sentinel*. Who knew what would be in the paper today, since the press had had all week to work on the sensational happenings in Oceanside?

The bells of St. Bridget's were chiming for eleven o'clock mass. Annie and her parents and Ethan would be there in their regular pew. I don't see Annie on Sundays. Her family is very big on togetherness, and Sunday is special and kept that way. It's nice. I wish and wish I had that kind of a family. Maybe if my mother had lived . . .

Charlie's parents would be at morning services too, worshipping in the church where their son had lain in state.

I thought about Lon. But I couldn't get Lon into any kind of focus. Right now he was a pile of ashes in a jar, or dust, scattered somewhere, drifting across other dust. I didn't think I'd like that for someone I loved. Dust wasn't something you could put back together again in your mind.

I cycled along Hudson, getting close to the 7-Eleven, and something was different. I stared at the store. It had its same-as-ever Sunday look with the blinds pulled down and the printed advertisements of last week's specials still showing in front of them. Maxwell House Coffee. Pillsbury Biscuits. The gate that's steel, or metal of some sort, was clamped in front of the door, the Closed sign was up, and I saw that the burglar alarm was unlit and quiet. So what was bugging me?

I was almost opposite the store before I realized. The newspaper racks had gone.

I got off my bike and peered at the ground. There'd been three racks: one for the *Sentinel*, one for the *Chronicle*, one for the *Tribune*. All three had vanished.

I walked around where they'd stood, scuffing my feet on the sidewalk. There were small square marks on the cement where the legs had been. The red post where they'd been chained was still there. But no racks. It was as if someone had come by in a big truck, stopped, sawed through the chain, lifted the racks, and driven away. Crazy! I felt totally disoriented. Those racks had been there for as long as I could remember.

I couldn't even think of another place to go to buy a paper. Why had they decided to move the racks? I walked up and down, still searching for them or for somebody to ask, and then I began thinking how dumb I must look. Once there had been a mailbox at the corner of Hudson and Mentor Avenues. They'd taken it away, and one day I saw an old guy standing there with a letter in his hand, looking bewildered and turning round and round like a dog chasing its tail. I'd thought it was pretty funny. I didn't think it was so funny now.

I stepped back and looked at the house where Big Eddie and Eddie Jr. live. It's right behind the store, but not attached. All the blinds were down there, too. Well, weird. I stood, wondering where to go next to get myself a *Sentinel*.

And then I noticed that a lot of cars were going past me, more than usual for a Sunday morning. I got back on my bike and rode slowly in the same direction.

Pretty soon I realized they were all headed for O-Hi, and when I got within eyeballing range, I saw a bunch of traffic in front of school. There couldn't be a game on. Anyway, it was too early. A blue van with KGIC on the side was parked under one of the trees and photographers with equipment, wires trailing, clustered on the grass by the front path. Another van with a television logo on the side came cruising up Hudson and stopped by the school gates. What was going on?

Everyone was staring up toward the tops of the trees, so I stared too, and there it was — the focus of all the attention. The school's name, Oceanside High, is printed out on big movable black letters on a glass notice board that towers over most of the buildings. The letters had been changed to read SUICIDE HIGH.

I stood, not believing. Some person or persons, under cover of darkness, had climbed a ladder and set to work. It hadn't been that hard. They'd used a lot of the original letters: the *S*; the *ICIDE*. To get the *U* they'd taken the top off the *O* and for the extra *I* they'd snipped away the bars of the *E*. That made a bigger gap between that first

I and the *C* than between the other letters so that it almost looked like three words: SUI CIDE HIGH. But nobody in a million years could make a mistake about what those words said. They were there, and someone had alerted the press.

"Jed!" Duane Watson was yelling at me from the front seat of a parked Datsun pickup. It's his brother Merv's truck, and Merv was driving. "Looks like we're going to have to change the name of the football team from the Chargers," Duane shouted. "Me and Merv got some good ideas. How about the Croakers? Or the Last Gaspers?"

"Funny stuff," I said coldly.

Duane drummed his fingers on the side of the Datsun, leaving clean blobs on the week's dust. "Hey, I didn't mean anything. It's just, this whole thing makes you kind of crazy."

Merv said something to him that I didn't get, then Duane yelled, "You *did* hear about Eddie Jr., didn't you?"

"Eddie Jr?" I instantly flashed to a picture of the 7-Eleven, the house with all the blinds pulled. "What about Eddie Jr.?"

"He swallowed a bunch of pills yesterday. He got them out of the shop when his old man wasn't looking."

That awful, fluttery coldness was back inside me. "Eddie Jr.?" I couldn't seem to get past repeating his name.

"He's still in the hospital, but he's going to be OK. They pumped out his stomach. Somebody said he only took baby aspirin and a bunch of E. T. kiddie vitamins because he likes the way they taste." Duane guffawed.

"Sometimes you're a turd, Watson," I said.

Duane's face froze. "Just bug off, Lennox."

I got on my bike and was out of there before I smacked him right on his ugly Adam's apple.

Eddie Jr.! Big old, simple old, Eddie Jr., who was always

smiling and trying to help, though his idea of helping could drive you out of your skull.

I was almost at the 7-Eleven. I saw the empty space where the paper racks had been, and I saw that there were some press trucks now, parked at the side of the house. Maybe someone had called them about Eddie Jr. too. A woman was just about ready to ring the doorbell. She wasn't Ellie Peck.

I slowed. Should I hang around, tell Big Eddie I was sorry and ... ?

The woman pulled down the jacket of her pale yellow suit, straightened her skirt. It wasn't the door that opened, though; it was the window on the second floor, and Big Eddie was leaning out.

"Go away," he said. "Haven't you people done enough?" He didn't shout. His voice wasn't that loud but I could hear every word.

"Oh, Mr. Sawyer ... there you are!" The woman had stepped back and was gazing up at the window.

Mr. Sawyer! I didn't even know big Eddie's name was Sawyer.

"I'm from Cable News," she called up. "The whole state wants to know about your son. How *is* Eddie Jr.? Is he going to be OK?"

"Go away," Big Eddie said again. His head pulled back like a turtle into its shell, and I saw that one of the TV photographers was still panning up at the now empty window. Another was taking pictures of the place where the newspaper racks had been.

"Wait, Mr. Sawyer! Wait just a minute!" Yellow Suit was getting frantic. "Just one question, OK? Then we'll go away."

Big Eddie's head reappeared in the window.

"Why did Eddie Jr...do what he did?" Yellow Suit asked delicately. "Was it in any way connected with the death of the congressman's son?"

"No. I'll tell you why my son did what he did." Big Eddie's words flowed like a river, flat and wide and deep, without even a ripple on the top.

"You came here, all of you. You came into our town. You were only doing your jobs, I knew that, and Jr. and I tried to help. He talked to you, and he said foolish things, and you encouraged him. He was pleased. Even though people laughed, he was pleased and happy because for the first time somebody was paying attention to him. Somebody was listening. But then you stopped with the questions, because he says the same thing over and over... that's the way he is. And that wasn't good copy."

Big Eddie leaned a little out of the window and spoke to a reporter who carried a notebook. "Are you getting all this down? Am I going slowly enough for you?"

The guy wasn't even writing.

"So then Jr. saw something that would work better," Big Eddie said. "If he killed himself like Charlie Curtis and the Lonnigan kid, he'd really be in the spotlight. Surefire, forever and ever attention. That's how dumb he is. He's so dumb he doesn't do much right, and that's why he's still alive. If he could, he'd be telling you all about it, trying to describe it, getting it wrong as usual."

I let out my breath. But he hadn't finished.

"You say you're only doing your job. And I'm saying OK, but there's something missing. And you don't even know what it is." His finger stabbed at Yellow Suit. "Do *you* know? Of course, you don't. Well, I'll tell you. You have no compassion. You can write headlines, you can't write caring."

111

"But Mr. Sawyer — are you really convinced that your son's suicide attempt and the death of congressman's . . . ?"

The window smashed down.

I pushed off on my bike. Get me away from here. Just away.

There's an alley between the 7-Eleven and the appliance store next door. As I cycled past, I saw that a lone photographer was perched on the edge of the big green trash container, taking pictures of the inside of the bin.

Without going closer I knew what was in there. I saw metal legs sticking in the air, the corner of what had once been a glass-fronted box. I imagined all the newspapers ripped apart, piled on top of each other in that smelly darkness.

No need to ask who'd done it. No need to ask why.

I did ask myself if Big Eddie would be in trouble for what he'd done to those racks and papers, and I knew he would. I knew, too, that he wouldn't care.

15

I went back home. It was Sunday, noon, and I didn't have a newspaper. What I had was plenty of time to think.

This whole thing seemed to me like one of those jumping firecrackers Charlie and I used to mess around with. We'd light one end of the string and stand back, and the sparks and fire would fizzle along, and pretty soon there'd be a pop, loud enough to scare us, and then the fizzle would run farther and there'd be another pop, louder than the first one, and Charlie and I would laugh and jump up and down. And then the red glow would spark along some more, and there'd be a terrific bang.

The only way to stop that firecracker once it started was to rush in, grab it, and throw it in a bucket of water. We always told ourselves that's what we'd do if things started to go wrong, because those jumpers can be dangerous. But we'd never had to stop one, and I'm not sure if either of us could have.

In Oceanside, someone or something had lit the fire-cracker fuse, and we'd already had the first explosions. But this time I didn't have a bucket of water, and I didn't know where to run to grab the firecracker to stop it from going even farther.

Charlie, Lon, Eddie Jr. Maybe Idris. Maybe Idris first. I sat at the table and drank powdered milk mixed with ice water because we were out of regular milk, and I'd forgotten to get some. And I made notes. They were the kind of notes you make when you have to do something, and you don't have the slightest idea what. When I'd finished, I crossed out the stuff that was no use to me and I was left with:

Find the second Gemini man. How? Where? (Check out Charlie's room, his locker stuff, the helmet.)
Try to talk to Lon's mother and see if Lon said anything to her.
Try finding out something more from Dominique or DD Hysinger.

Dominique seemed an easier nut to crack.

At the beginning of the list I'd written a message to my-self and underlined it three times.

When Eddie Jr. is back in circulation, go into the 7-Eleven and ask him for an apple. Talk to him. Be his friend.

I looked again at my list. First things first. OK, look some more for Gemini man.

It was 12:30 P.M., and I thought Charlie's family should be home from church. I called, got Dave, and asked to speak to Evelyn. We talked a bit. I said I guessed it had been bad today in church without Charlie, and she said real bad and that the congregation had decided to buy a bunch of reference books for writers and give them to the Oceanside Library in his memory. I said that was nice.

"Did you hear about Eddie Jr.?" Evelyn asked.

"Yeah."

"And the notice board?"

"I saw it," I said, and then I asked if I could come over.

"I'm looking for something, Evelyn. If I find it I may get a few answers. Charlie's room is the only place I can think to check. I especially need to go through the stuff that was taken from his locker."

"You want to look today?"

"Could you sneak me in? I hate to be hassling you on Sunday, but I'm real antsy. Nothing's coming together, you know? It's just one thing after another. But I don't want to run into your parents. They've had enough."

Evelyn was quiet for a few seconds.

"Come on over, Jed. We'll all be in the dining room. The front door will be open. Just be quiet when you're upstairs. My mother's awful nervous."

"Thanks, Evelyn. I'll be quiet. Is . . . is his helmet there?"

"Yes. Take it, Jed."

The helmet was the first thing I looked at when I got upstairs. But there was no note.

I spent close to an hour in Charlie's room. It hadn't been touched, and all his things lay around the way he'd left them. It hurt to put my hands on them, to go through the drawers of his desk, to check the carton that held his notebook and the rest of his stuff from school. I was real careful, shaking out all the books, flipping through for a message in the margin, and all the time I was worrying that maybe his mother would come up, and wondering what she would say if she saw me rooting around.

Once feet did come up the stairs, heavy feet that had to be Dave's, and I froze. But he went in the bathroom and then thumped back down again. I tried to hurry things up, but I had to stop a couple of times and stare out the window and swallow my tears. There was no way not to think about death that afternoon. Not there, in Charlie's room.

I searched everywhere. I found nothing. No reason, no hint of dark secrets, no Gemini man; I went away disappointed and frustrated.

On the way home I had another idea, and I veered onto Rio Grande. When Charlie and I were little, there was a wall that ran between an old house and an empty, weedgrown lot. We'd climbed that wall plenty of times and jumped off it. Once we'd discovered a loose brick and many a Gemini man note had rested in the spidery space behind it.

I found the place. There was no old house now, no empty lot. Only an Econo Service Station in a sea of blank concrete. Two locked up rest rooms stood where the wall used to be.

I cycled back to the bungalow and slumped again at the table where my list still lay. Gemini man, where are you? Where did you put him, Charlie, and why were you so clever about it? We never hid our notes this well before.

I couldn't face any more of the powdered milk so I had some of our famous sugar-free water from the faucet while I considered the next two things on my list. Try to talk to Lon's mother. Try to find out something more from Dominique.

I swirled the ice in my glass the way Dominique had done and thought how I could just pick up the phone and call her and say, "Hey, Dom, how about taking a ride out to McCormack Beach?" I had a feeling she'd say yes. Not that I think I'm so great. But Dom wants something from me, information she thinks I have that I don't. And I want something from her. I want information I'm sure she *does* have.

She'd go out there in her little car. Heck, she might even drive me. So suppose somebody did see us? I'm white, after all, not black like Charlie. I'm OK to be seen with.

She'd spread that tricky little blanket she keeps in the back, and we'd sit down. She'd be wearing a pair of those real short white shorts she has and maybe one of those skimpy crop tops that leaves half of her belly bare. In front the shorts are OK, but in back they're more than OK. They show the beginnings of those pale round half-moons. Shoot, I'd never realized that I'd noticed the way Dominique's shorts were in back, but I guess I had. Yesterday, in the ocean, I'd slid my hands down the cool wetness of Annie, the round firmness.

I stood up, walked into the kitchen, and junked the rest of my ice. Then I took one of the cubes and held it against my neck. Hormones on the rampage are certainly powerful stuff. I tried to remember when mine had started getting out of control. Probably when I first saw Annie, when I first touched her.

I grabbed up more of the ice.

When I calmed down some, I decided that today talking to Lon's mother would be my best bet. I went back in the living room, got my box of photographs, emptied it, and pawed around till I found the picture of her dead son — the one where he looked so alive and so innocent. I put it in an envelope.

This time I took the Honda though, because Lon lives clear on the other side of town. Did live. The address had been in the paper Mrs. Sanchez had given me, and I found the house easily. It was a white colonial, prim and proper with a green trim. The drapes were tied back, each one as neat and careful as in a kid's drawing of a house. I put the Honda in slow and rolled to a stop at the end of the driveway.

The door had a polished brass eagle for a knocker. Representative Lonnigan's wife's house. Lon's house. Who'd have thought when he staggered into school every morning that he'd come from a place like this? I glanced down at the envelope before I lifted the eagle knocker and let it drop. What an intrusion! What a nerve! Well, maybe no one would open the door.

Someone did, a girl of about twelve. She had brown hair and a speckling of freckles, like Lon's.

"Hi," I said.

"Hi."

"I went to school with your brother," I said. "I guess you're Lon's sister?"

She nodded.

"Is your mom home? I have something for her."

"What?" She didn't open the door any wider.

"It's a picture of Lon. I thought she might want to have it." The words were true, but I felt like a liar as I looked into the girl's suspicious blue eyes.

"This isn't a trick? You're not from one of those papers?"

"No. Honest. I'm not."

"Were you a friend of Lonnie's?"

I struggled with that one, too, and then I said, "I knew him. Look."

I edged the corner of the photograph from the envelope, and she gave a little hiccupy gulp. "I guess you'd better come in."

118

Geez! And I'd called Duane Watson a turd.

I stood in the hallway that had black-and-white squares on the floor, like some sort of giant checkerboard, while she yelled "Mom. There's someone to see you" and disappeared up the stairs.

I smoothed my hair and wished I'd taken time to find a less wrinkled and ratty-looking T-shirt. A huge grandfather clock beside me had a pendulum that was as big as a Frisbee. You could get hypnotized from just watching that pendulum swing, but I didn't have time to test it out, because a woman came through a swinging door to the side. I got a whiff of food cooking. Sunday lunch.

The woman was small, with light hair and a pointy chin that she cocked up at me. "You wanted to see me?"

I handed her the envelope, wishing I hadn't come. Wasn't there some saying about letting sleeping dogs lie? Well, Charlie and Lon were both sleeping, that was for sure. I was feeling the way I'd felt with Idris's mother. To her, Idris had been Baby Iris. To this woman, Lon was probably Lonnie or that other name he had — James, Jamie, her darling son. To me he was somebody to be sorry about, somebody who'd died and mysteriously turned into dust. But what he *really* was to me was a step to understanding Charlie's death.

I shifted from one foot to the other as she looked at the picture. "I'm with the school paper...." Oops, I shouldn't have said that. No newspaper stuff. "I mean, I take pictures for the yearbook. I took this one a couple of months ago."

Her head came up. "Do *you* know why he did it? *Do* you?"

I didn't mean to take a step backward. "No. Not really."

"What do you mean, not really?"

"I . . . he told me once that he . . . 'saw her face.' It seemed to mean something to him. But it didn't mean anything to me."

The dark circles under her eyes were almost translucent, deep blue and shiny, like the sea. "Wait here," she said. "No." Her hand waved toward an open door. "Go in there and sit down."

She was already racing up the wide staircase. I stood for a minute where she'd left me, then went into the living room and sat on a peach-colored velvet couch.

When she came back, I saw that she didn't have the envelope with the photograph. Instead she carried a folded piece of paper. She sat beside me on the couch.

"This is the note he left. I haven't made it public, and I'm trusting you not to. I'm showing it to you because there's something in here about 'her face' and maybe you can help me understand."

I moved to the edge of the couch, and before I could open the paper I had to wipe my suddenly sweaty hands on my T-shirt. There was something in here. Something important.

The page had been ripped from a notebook and the words scrawled across the paper were in big, big letters that fell off the ends of the lines. "I SAW PEACE. IT WAS IN HER FACE BEFORE WE DROPPED HER OVER THE EDGE OF THE WORLD. I WANT . . ."

The word *want* ended at the margin, and nothing followed it. I turned the paper over and looked at the back, half expecting in some crazy way that there'd be a Gemini man. But it wasn't Lon who'd known about Gemini man, and there was nothing more. God! There was enough.

"I suppose what he wanted was peace too." Mrs. Lonnigan pulled at her fingers, tugging as if trying to pull them

120

out of their sockets. "But whose face? It must have been one of those drug people. Do you know?"

I shook my head. But I *did* know. I didn't want to, but I did. A girl had disappeared. A girl had been dropped over the Edge of the World. I knew, and my heart thumped in time with the tick of the big clock.

"He took an overdose, you know. Four different kinds of drugs. Four. Some he swallowed, and some he injected." Pull, pull, pull on her fingers. I thought I could hear the bones parting. "Looking for peace. I guess that's what he was doing. Everybody back there knew him. Everybody in Washington. I had him in a place for a while, you know, a treatment place? When we moved I thought, nice little town, new chance, new life. It didn't take him long to find his own kind."

I wanted to say something in Lon's defense, but I couldn't frame the words. When you come new, it's hard to crack the groups in school. The jocks, the soshes, the small twos and threes that have hung around together for years. But if you do dope, you're in with one group, no problem.

Mrs. Lonnigan was still talking, whispering actually. "I wondered sometimes if he got into drugs to spite his father. I don't know."

I tried deep breathing but it didn't do any good.

"I'm sorry she's gone," Charlie had told Mrs. Dellarosa. And he hadn't meant "gone" as in "gone to San Francisco." I had a quick flashback of me asking Glenn Ponderelli, way back, "What do you mean, Charlie's dead?"

"He's dead. As in deceased, defunct, croaked," Glenn had answered.

Idris was dead as in gone. Gone to heaven. Gone to hell. Gone from the planet Earth. Somehow she'd died on them, and they'd dropped her over the Edge of the World. Lon and who else? I was about ready to jump out of my skin.

Mrs. Lonnigan was still talking in that hoarse whisper. "I protected him at the end, though. I protected his father, too, heaven knows why. Accidental death, they ruled it. How do you take that much stuff accidentally? I guess some people can. I think the police knew. They were nice to me though."

One of her poor, hurting fingers flicked at the note. "Can you imagine what those people from the papers would have done with this? Drugs, drugs, and more drugs. Dropping over the Edge of the World. Helping each other drop out. 'Lucy in the sky with diamonds.' Is that the only way to peace?"

She stopped and in the silence the grandfather clock chimed the half hour.

I knew that the "Edge of the World" meant nothing to her. It probably would have to the cops, if she'd shown them this. The cops are pretty hip to the terms the kids use. But to Mrs. Lonnigan it wasn't a place, it was another of those weird drug terms. But it *was* a place, a place with a long, long fall where a body would never be seen because it would disappear into that thick springy brush, among all the trash, the junked old mattresses and couches and filth of Oceanside. Turkey buzzards sometimes circle above the Edge of the World. I felt a weak wash of sickness.

"Do *you* do drugs?" Mrs. Lonnigan asked.

I shook my head and put Lon's note carefully on the couch between us.

"That's good. Don't. Don't ever."

"No. I won't. I stood up and began edging away.

She was still sitting there as I walked backward across

the black-and-white tiles, going jerkily like some very scared puppet, getting myself out of there.

"Thank you for the photograph," she called.

"You're welcome."

The last thing I heard was the crack, crack, crack as she began pulling on her fingers again.

16

I rode up to Chitney Trail and got off the bike at the Edge
of the World. Everything was Sunday afternoon quiet.
Birds sang a sleepy chorus. A burnt orange butterfly set-
tled on a cluster of white shrubs, the small blossoms drifting down like snow. I thought maybe it was a monarch
butterfly. Pretty soon now all the monarchs would be on
their way south to Pismo Beach to hang in the tall trees.
I'd gone down last year with Charlie to see them and we'd
walked under the pines, but we'd only seen four butterflies
the whole day. I guess the others had moved on, and those
four got left behind.

I examined this monarch as if I'd never seen any kind of
butterfly in all my life . . . its beautiful ragged edges, the
dark circles like eyes on the wings, the way it folded to
become a leaf, then opened itself again to the sunshine.
I didn't want to think about anything else except the
beauty of the butterfly. I didn't want to think of death —
Lon Lonnigan's, Charlie Curtis's. The near miss of Eddie

124

Jr. Most of all I didn't want to think of what lay at the bottom of this cliff.

After a while I picked up an empty Perrier bottle that some classy person had thrown from a car, and I leaned out and let it drop from my hand. It fell without a sound; there was no tinkle of glass as it landed. But Idris would have been heavier than a Perrier bottle. There would have been a thump, and for sure it would have taken more than one person to get her over, one at the head, one at the feet. Unless somebody rolled her. Oh, God! I couldn't bear to think about that.

I paced the cliff edge, looking for a way down, but there wasn't any. I'd known that before I started pacing, and I was glad. I didn't want to go searching down there.

You could get in, though, by walking the four miles from Water Creek. A couple of years ago a car went over the Edge of the World, and the firemen and cops had beaten their way back using scythes and machetes. They'd thought somebody might still be inside, but the car was empty. It turned out it had been stolen down in San Jose. They could go in again now and look for Idris.

I'd have to call them.

"You'll promise to tell me before you do anything." Dominique's voice. "We need to be sure it's right for Charlie."

Charlie couldn't be mixed up in this. But somebody had thrown Idris over. Lon and who?

"I thought you and Charlie used to meet up at Chitney Trail, Dominique," I'd said.

"Not anymore."

Of course not anymore. Considering what was down there.

Over and over I told myself that Charlie couldn't have known. And over and over I came up with the same answer. He'd gone to Idris's mother, tears in his eyes. He'd said he was sorry. Then he'd killed himself. Wise up, Lennox. Charlie was involved all right.

A small station wagon filled with kids bumped across the grass. It had a sunroof and a girl was standing up, the top half of her above the car, her long, red hair whipping out behind her.

"Hi," she called. "You look lonesome. Want to party?"

The car slowed to cruising and from inside someone yelled, "You gonna jump? Go ahead. Might as well be in fashion, man!"

I began running toward them, screaming like a madman, and for a second I saw the startled faces, the open mouths, and then the car swung around fast, the brakes sliding in the dry grass. The girl was almost jerked out.

I was just about to it, my hands reaching for the back fender. If I could have caught that station wagon, I'd have ripped it apart. But all I managed to do was thump the back and scream words at them I didn't even know I knew.

The girl yelled something back at me, something about cooling it, and was I a moron or what? And then I was standing again in the birdsong silence, listening to my own ragged breathing, listening to myself sob.

I don't know how long it was before I got on the Honda and rode to Dominique's.

I guess Sunday is Estella the maid's day off. When I rang the bell, it was a tall, bald guy in white tennis shorts and shirt who opened the door. A section of the Sunday paper dangled in his hand. I knew him by sight — the big old wine maker, Dominique's father.

"Hi," I said. "Is Dom here?"

His eyes checked out my wrinkled J. C. Penney T-shirt, my faded red shorts, my sneakers with no socks.

126

"My name's Jed," I said. "I know her from school."

He looked past me to the motorbike, and it wasn't hard to guess what he thought of me. Not much. He jerked his head toward the hall behind him. "She's out by the pool. You can go through the French doors, then make a left past the courts."

"Thanks."

"What did you say your name was again?"

"Jed Lennox."

He nodded and stood aside to let me walk around him. Papa Bear. The one who could never, ever, under any circumstances be allowed to know about his daughter Dominique and Charlie. What if he found out that Dom was mixed up in . . . what? A murder? Anyway, a death.

She was lying on one of those canvas circles that look like a trampoline, spread out on her stomach. I saw her through the wire fence, and when I opened the gate, she turned her head and then quickly sprang up.

"Jed! Terrific!"

Her swimsuit was the kind that's cut high on the top of the thighs so her legs seemed as long as Annie's. It clung to her like the skin on a grape and it was grape-colored too, a deep, dusky purple.

She padded toward me. "My father let you through the sacred portals?" She rolled her eyes. "And me here without a chaperone? Maybe he's getting soft, but I doubt it."

There was sweat on her face, and her hair was a damp, dark gold. She was standing so close that I could feel the humidity coming from her, the warmth below the wetness.

"I'm so glad you came, Jed. I was bored to death today. And if there's one thing I hate, it's to be bored."

I didn't see her move closer, but I felt the rise in the humidity. "I try to be always on the edge of disaster, especially with Pop," she said. "Doing things that would make

127

him absolutely furious...but making sure he doesn't know."

"And you get away with it? I hear your father's a pretty sharp guy."

"He's sharp about most things. Which makes it even better when I pull something off. Then it's one in the eye for him, and I score." She made a couple of fake boxer jabs at my chest. "Pow! Pow! It's my game, you know?"

I'd guessed. Like meeting Charlie up on Chitney Trail or out at McCormack. And her knowing that every time they did it together was one in the eye for dear old dad. Her game.

"I'm sorry you were bored today," I said. "But cheer up. I'm here to unbore you."

The purple eyes widened. "Don't tell me something else awful has happened. I heard about poor Eddie Jr."

"Something else *has* happened. I found out where Idris is."

I'd promised myself that I'd take a mind picture of Dominique the second I said those words and that what I'd see on her face, and examine now and later, would be some kind of proof. But I didn't need to take a picture.

The pinkness went from her cheeks as if wiped away by a washcloth. "Isn't...isn't she in San Francisco?"

"No. She's down at the bottom of the Edge of the World."

"I try to be always on the edge of disaster," Dominique had said. Right. The Edge of the World. I watched as she covered her face with her hands. And I waited.

In a few seconds she opened her fingers and stared through them. "No," she whispered. "No."

"Don't give me that, Dominique. You knew. Charlie knew."

"Look, Jed." She reached out and took my hand. "Please. Come and sit. We need to talk."

I let her lead me to a glass-topped table under a yellow umbrella and sat, because yes, we needed to talk. There was a plastic bottle of suntan lotion on the table, and she turned it round and round, not meeting my eyes. Her words came hesitantly.

"You're wrong. I didn't know. I swear to you. I swear, I didn't know Idris was down there. But I suspected that something had happened with her and Charlie. Because he talked about how awful it was when she vanished. And that's when he began acting so strange. I told you. No lovemaking. No happiness. One day he said, 'There's so little between being alive and being dead. Just one small breath.' " She darted a quick glance at me and then down again. "He came out with that in the middle of one of his long silences."

The suntan-lotion bottle skidded away from her, and I rescued it and held it so she had nothing to take her attention from me.

"Afterwards, well, I thought he'd been talking about himself. About what he planned to do."

I swallowed, pushing away the image of Charlie hanging from the rope, the sudden crack when his neck snapped, that quick instant difference between Charlie alive and Charlie dead. I shook my head. No. No! "What did you think *then*, though, Dominique, when he first said it?"

"I didn't pay much attention. Charlie was all the time talking weird stuff. It could have been something from a story he was writing or thinking about. You know how he was."

I knew. He'd gaze into space. He wouldn't answer when you spoke. I didn't like Dominique. I didn't know how

Charlie could have loved her. But maybe I believed her on this.

"Now that I've told you Idris is down there, do you think he was talking about her? About how she was alive, and he pushed her over and then she was dead?"

"Jed!" Dominique shoved back her chair and stood, almost knocking over the umbrella. "Why are you saying such awful things? Charlie could have *known*, somehow. That doesn't mean he *did* it."

"Just knowing Idris was dead made him kill himself? Come on, Dominique."

Her voice was shaky. "Why are you questioning me like this anyway? I've told you all I can. And I warned you not to rush around talking if you found something. That's all Charlie's parents would need — to have some kind of awful suspicion thrown on him. And Charlie" — she wiped at her eyes — "hasn't he paid the price for whatever it was, whatever he knew? If *she's* dead and he's dead too, what good will it do? Let them rest in peace."

"What about Idris's mother? Doesn't she have a right to know? Doesn't Idris have a right to be buried and have prayers said over her like anyone else? It's not that simple, Dominique."

I set the lotion in the middle of the table and stood too. Dominique turned her back to me, and I thought I heard a little sob. The chair webbing had left tracks, crisscrossing the backs of her legs, and the swimsuit had crept up the way her shorts do, but I scarcely noticed. Even rampant hormones simmer down when you're thinking about deaths . . . about suicides and, maybe, murders.

Now I definitely heard a sob.

"I can't put this together properly," I muttered. "What I really need is the other Gemini man. Then I'll know what Charlie wanted me to do."

Dominique swung around. "You need who?" Sharp little voice. Sharp little eyes. It was strange. I'd been believing her in a lot of this, but those eyes and that voice pulled me out of it.

"I have to go, Dom. I can find the way out myself."

Her father met me in the hallway and opened the front door for me. His timing was so perfect I wondered if he'd been keeping an eye on us through the glass of the French doors. I also wondered which one of his four wives had been Dominique's mother, and if it was because of her that Dominique hated him so much.

"How are the grapes coming?" I asked him.

"I think we'll have an excellent yield," he said, and we nodded seriously at one another as if the most important thing in the world was the quality of the wine he'd be bottling a couple of years down the line.

"Has all this commotion at the school ended?" he asked. "If I thought there'd be more, I'd take Dominique away from there quicker than a cat can spit."

"That would be pretty quick," I said, and he nodded seriously again and closed the door.

17

I did a lot of thinking on Sunday night, but I still wasn't sure what to do. I had to tell about Idris. I didn't have to tell about Idris. Maybe the firecracker had fizzled itself out in the middle of the string and telling about Idris would be like putting another match to it and standing back, waiting for the next bang. There were some facts I couldn't get away from, though. Charlie and Idris and Lon were dead. No new information would bring them back. But to hide the truth . . . to hide a body . . . what would that make me?

On Monday morning I decided to put off the decision till that night. I put off the decision on telling Annie, too. Tell one, tell all, and I wasn't sure yet how I felt about that. So I met Annie as usual, and we rode to school, and I stayed quiet.

Mr. Haig, the janitor had been busy with the notice board. He'd taken down Suicide High, found the discarded *A* and *N* and the bars of the *E*, but the top of the *O* was still missing.

"Uceanside High?" I asked Annie. But neither of us thought it was funny.

I guess there'd been a lot of high-level consultations over the weekend. A peer counseling group was in the works so "Students can relate to other students and talk about their problems before they're driven to extremes."

We all knew what *to extremes* meant.

There'd been an editorial in the Sunday *Sentinel* suggesting we import a guy from Los Angeles who's an expert on teen suicide. He goes around schools, showing slides of kids who've killed themselves by stabbing or shooting . . . or hanging. I knew already I'd never be able to look at the hanging slide. He has pictures of what happens in an emergency room when they're pumping out somebody's stomach, when tubes are stuck up the nose, sucking out all the junk that's been swallowed. I guess poor old Eddie Jr. had that done to him.

Eddie Jr.'s father had been wrong on one count, though. There was an article in one of the Santa Rosa papers that was so filled with caring that it made my throat hurt:

> There has to be help for our young people. They're facing the kind of problems we never dreamed of. Their pain is real, and it needs to be taken seriously. Suicide comes only when all hope is gone. We must offer them hope before it's too late.

It was already too late, of course, for two of the kids of Oceanside High.

Somebody said Eddie Jr. was getting out of the hospital this afternoon and that he was OK.

"How would they know old Oofy-Goofy was OK anyway?" Duane Watson asked. "His head's so messed up to begin with, who'd know the difference?"

133

"Why don't you lay off, Watson," Bob Rothman said. "You've got about as much sensitivity as a brick wall."

I'd had enough, and I did what I'd been wanting to do for a while. I grabbed a handful of Duane's T-shirt and pushed my face into his. "Yeah. Lay off with the Oofy-Goofy stuff or *your* head's going to be so messed up you'll never get it together again."

Duane wriggled free. "Lay off *yourself,* man. *You* weren't so sensitive with your friend Curtis. Weren't you two supposed to be real tight?" Duane straightened his T-shirt. "How come you didn't get to *him* before he was driven to those 'extremes?' "

"Shut up, you bonehead." My voice was rising, but somewhere in my mind a little voice taunted and prodded. You *should* have gotten to Charlie. The truth hurts, and you know it.

Bob put a hand on my arm. "A bunch of us are going over to Eddie's on Wednesday after school to play Fish with him. Fish is his favorite game. You want to come?"

"Sure," I muttered. "I'll come."

After school I walked Annie to the park. "Are you going to the lab?" she asked.

"Yes. But I'm heading home first. I've got some pictures of Charlie his parents haven't seen. I want to get them and make copies. Then I'll put an album together for the Curtises."

"Nice Jed!" Annie gave me a quick skim of a kiss, and I stood, peering through the mesh wire like a monkey in the zoo while she went in the locker room and changed into her blue swimsuit. Then I watched her walk across the cement, all long brown legs and long, swinging black hair. I put a few palm trees in the background, added a flower behind her ear and a flower bracelet circling her ankle, and I took the kind of picture you see on the front of a travel magazine. COME TO TAHITI.

Oh, Annie, you are so beautiful it makes me hurt. I didn't want to stop looking at her. I didn't want to go home. Most of all, I didn't want to have to make decisions about decisions. "Nice Jed," she'd said. I wasn't so sure.

Back in the bungalow I sorted negatives, comparing them with the proof sheets, picking the best. But I couldn't keep my mind on what I was doing. Instead, I conjured up a picture of Idris, the way I used to see her slinking along the hallway in school. Then I saw shadowy, faceless figures standing on the cliff's edge, swinging her like a jumprope. A brightening sky — Charlie's face. No. No. I found a picture of him in junior high. He was wearing the mirrored sunglasses that were big then, and there I was, camera in hand, reflected in the lenses. It was a real state-of-the-art shot, no question. I'd won thirty bucks with it. Dad was away, and I'd blown the loot on carryout chicken and ribs and tutti-frutti salad. Charlie came over, and we lay around playing the game of imagining the pictures to go along with the words coming from Mr. Yamamoto's TV.

"Now he's kissing her," Charlie had said.

"Uh-uh. No way. Tough detectives don't kiss, not this early in the movie. She has her back turned is all, and he's searching the drawer in her desk."

I remember Mr. Yamamoto changed channels in the middle, and Charlie ran over and asked him to put it back because we were listening.

"The one who came over," Mr. Yamamoto had said, nodding his head. And suddenly the words were spinning around like a carousel inside my brain. "The one who came over. The one who came over." Did he mean, then, that day? Sometimes? Or did he mean another time, a time I didn't even know about. Did he mean to his bungalow or ours? What *did* he mean? I stood up, and my legs were shaking. I put the picture I'd been studying on the pile, and I went out and stepped across to Mr. Yamamoto's porch.

He was astonished to see me. Face it, we don't usually call on him, and he doesn't usually call on us. Through his half-open door I could see a bare living room, one chair, a television set even bigger than ours. On the screen, Phil Donahue was talking to a guy dressed in women's clothes.

"Yes, Mr. Lennox?" Mr. Yamamoto asked.

"May I speak to you? It's important."

"Certainly. You come in."

We stood just inside the door.

"It's about my friend Charlie. 'The one who came over'?"

I pushed my hands deep in my pockets to keep them from trembling. "When did he come over last? Can you remember?"

"Certainly. Was the afternoon of the night he died. Saturday." Behind Mr. Yamamoto's glasses, his eyes blinked and blinked.

"He came here?"

"Not here. He came to your house, Mr. Lennox."

I tried to keep my voice steadier than my hands. "I wasn't home?"

"No. Nobody home. He knock many times. He have something for you. I come out and say I take for you. But your friend, he says no. He will wait. I give him the key." Mr. Yamamoto blinked some more. "Was OK?"

"Yes. Sure. So he went in. How long did he wait?"

Mr. Yamamoto held up one finger, then added another. "Two minutes. Then he get on the Honda and leave."

On the TV, Phil Donahue said something, and the audience laughed and laughed.

"Did you see what it was he had for me? Did he take it with him when he left?"

"It was big envelope." Mr. Yamamoto drew a square in the air with his index fingers. "This size. Brown. He not take it when he go. You not find?"

The carousel was whirling again inside my head, turning faster and faster. "No. I didn't find it. I'll go look now. Thanks, Mr. Yamamoto." I backed out, and he gave me his funny little bow and closed the door behind me. I jumped from porch to porch and stood in our living room, staring around in a daze. Where had Charlie left the envelope?

I tried to think back to that Saturday that seemed so long ago. I'd been ice skating with Annie. When I got home around five, my father was there. He'd looked up and grunted. He was sitting in his chair, the table beside him piled high with magazines and circulars, papers strewn on the floor. I camera panned around the room now, remembering, looking for the envelope. But it wasn't there.

I advanced the film to Sunday. Still a mess. My father cramming all the stuff he was taking with him into his ratty old dufflebag, carrying loads out to the camper, neither of us talking. The Sunday *Sentinel* lay scattered across his chair when he left.

I closed my eyes, concentrating. I'd gone over to Mrs. Sanchez's for dinner. We'd had gazpacho, and we'd talked about my mother, the way we do a lot of the time. I'm greedy for talk about her, but I always end up sad.

"I tell you and tell you," Mrs. Sanchez said. "She want you bad. She know she take risk. You face your father. You ask him right out."

"I don't want to ask him anything. I'm scared to ask him. He'd tell me, in all the gory detail."

Mrs. Sanchez reached across the table and touched my

hand. "When you were little, Jed, you always think a monster live in your closet. You won't let me open the door to show you no. Then one night you open it yourself. Poof!" Mrs. Sanchez threw up her hands. "No monster. Then you believe. No monster here either, Jed. Her death not your fault."

Not my fault either that I'd lost what Charlie left.

OK. Back to Monday morning. There I am, getting up early, shoveling all the papers together, dumping them on the floor of the service porch, getting the vacuum, changing the sheets. Wait, rewind. Play that over.

A minute or so later I was down on my knees in the service porch, pawing through what I'd piled there on Monday. Circulars, ads, unopened sweepstake envelopes, hunting and fishing catalogs, throw-away supermarket fliers. I tossed them aside, burrowing, sifting like a miner looking for gold. And there it was. The big, brown envelope. From the corner where the stamp should have been Gemini man stared sightlessly up at me.

18

The envelope was closed with a metal hook. I opened the prongs, pulled out the contents, and counted rapidly; there were eight pages. A paper clip joined a white envelope to the first page. Typed on the envelope were the words, "Jed, please read my note to you last."

I was still on my knees in the service porch when the phone rang. I got up and carried the typed pages and the note with me inside the house. My hands were clammy as I picked up the receiver, and already I was reading the title and the first few lines of Charlie's story. For of course it was a story. What else should I have expected from a writer?

I cleared my throat and spoke into the phone. "Yeah? Hello."

"Jed?"

It was Dominique.

"Jed? About Charlie. Can't we just ..."

"Not now, Dominique," I said, and hung up the phone.

In another moment I was sitting at the table with the pages in front of me. The title was in capitals. DARKS UNDREAMED OF. I read.

My name is Charlie. I am seventeen years old. I am black. My girl friend's name is Dominique. She's beautiful, she's rich, and she's white. Do you sense trouble immediately? You're right.

We'd meet, my Dominique and I, secretly and by night because what other way is there in a small town like ours where her Daddy is powerful and prejudiced? We'd go to a high meadow that we knew of and in the dusk that smelled of grass and flowers, we'd lie on a blanket and make the sweetest love, and talk about how I'd be rich and famous someday and how we'd leave this town and live together, happy forever and ever. The dreams. The lies.

One night, as we lay close, I heard a rustling in the woods that bordered our meadow. How did I hear anything, I wonder now, with Dominique's body so tight against mine, with Dominique's breath in my mouth and the scents of her filling my soul, when it was such a small noise, no more than a whisper of sound?

I eased myself from the pull of Dominique's arms, and I went in the woods, and by the light from my flashlight and the three-quarter moon I saw the girl. She lay against a tree trunk, her legs apart, her eyes glazed. I knew her. Her name was Idris, and she was a senior at the school Dominique and I attended. Let's say that we didn't mix with the same people or get our pleasures from the same sources. Idris was an addict, a semiamateur prostitute and Main Lady to DD Hysinger, the school drug dealer.

I stopped reading, imagining Charlie staring out of his window, the way he did when he was writing a story, and

140

all the time knowing that he'd be leaving this behind, that when I read it, or someone read it, he'd be dead.

I could see that Hysinger's main lady was very ill. There was sweat on her skin, and her face was the green color that you sometimes see on the underside of a spring leaf. I knelt beside her and spoke her name. Her eyes opened. She said something and groaned. If I hadn't been so close to her, I would never have heard the words.

"Got me some bad stuff," she whispered and her head rolled on her neck and was still, like a broken-down windup toy.

There was a red scarf with gold zodiac signs on it tied round her head, gypsy fashion. It had slipped sideways, and I eased it off and used it to wipe away the sweat, then dropped it close to her hand. Her fingers clawed around it.

"I'm going for help," I said. "I'll be right back."

I ran, then, to where I'd left Dominique.

She'd gathered up her blanket, and she stood clutching it bunched up against her.

"Somebody's sick back there," I yelled. "Find her and stay with her. I'm going for help." Did I already say that I have a motorbike, a Honda, and that Dominique has a car and that we'd come separately to this place? Already I was racing for the bike, but Dominique was calling, "Wait a second, Charlie. Wait! Who is it?" She must have moved quickly, because she was all at once between me and the bike, grabbing for my arm.

"Look," I said, "we don't have time. It's Idris Dellarosa from school." I pried Dominique's fingers from my arm.

"What do you mean you're going for help? And asking me to stay here? Are you crazy? Everyone will know we've been together."

It was one of those moments in time when the decision one makes can affect life ever after. But I didn't know that then. Now I realize all the things I should have done. I should have pushed Dominique aside. I should have knocked her down if I had to. But I didn't. Maybe I couldn't even do that now, even now, knowing all I know about the ever after. I hesitated.

"She can't be *that* bad," Dominique urged. "Leave her alone. She'll be OK. Everybody gets sick."

"She's *real* sick, Dominique."

We stood listening. There was no sound now but the sighing of the wind in the tall trees. I began running back into the woods, and Dominique came slowly behind.

Idris hadn't moved. I leaned down and touched her face. It was cold and damp and her eyes didn't open, not even when I whispered her name. I put my fingers on her throat at the place where you check the pulse. There was no pulse.

Behind me, Dominique said, "She's sleeping. She'll be OK when she wakes up. Let's get out of here."

"She's dead," I said.

Dominique took a quick step backward. "She can't be. Don't be so . . ."

"Let me have your blanket, Dominique. I have to cover her. Then you leave. Nobody needs to stay with her now. I can head right for the police station."

Dominique clutched her blanket as if it were a life-jacket. "You are totally out of your mind. You want to use my blanket to cover a dead person? So somebody can trace it back to me? Oh, sure, Charlie. Great idea!"

I didn't watch as she stumbled away. Instead I stood looking down at Idris. She had the most peaceful, serene expression, as if she'd looked at death and found it better than her earthly life. She still held the scarf.

My own hands were clenched on the edge of the table, my arms rigid. I made myself relax and flex my fingers. "Maybe he saw her face. Her face was nice." Peace. Poor dead Idris. Poor dead Lon. Poor dead Charlie.

I thought Dominique had taken off, but she was waiting for me by her car. "What are you going to do?" she asked.

"Get on my bike and bring somebody up here."

"Look, darling . . ." She came close to me. "Please, please don't. There'll be police. They'll find out you were here with me. They always find out stuff like that. My father . . ." Tears spilled from her eyes. "Please don't. If Idris is dead, what difference can it make? Let someone else find her. Pretend it never happened. Pretend we never saw her."

I knew that for the rest of my life I'd know I'd seen her. But Dominique was right in one way. There was nothing we could do except get involved. It's easy to rationalize. At that moment, standing with Dominique, and later, sitting stunned in my room, I thought I could live with letting it go. I couldn't, of course.

It began to rain that night. I heard the rain start and I visualized it dripping through the trees, filling up the edges of those dead eyes, washing that dead face, and I couldn't bear it. I should at least have spread the scarf over her face. Why hadn't I? Was I too scared? Too anxious to get away?

I had no idea what I was going to do when I got out of bed, put on my oilskins, got the flashlight, and took off. Our bathroom light went on as I wheeled my bike out of the yard, and I was worried that I'd wakened someone, Mom maybe. She'd look and find my empty bed, and she'd remember how strange that was when the news came out about the dead girl. What if she thought I'd killed her? It was a ridiculous idea, but it frightened me. Not that my mother would think that, but that someone else might if I told. Idris went to my school. What had I been doing up there on the high meadow? Was I alone? I'm black. That isn't a factor, I know. But when you are black, it occurs to you.

I rode the trail to the high meadow. My feet and the bottoms of my legs were soaked, and I squished when I got down from the bike and walked through the wet grass. My flashlight shone on the gleaming leaves, arched rainbows in the mist.

Laughter exploded next door from Mr. Yamamoto's TV, and a voice that I knew was Phil Donahue's asked. "But which bathroom do you use when you go out to dinner? The men's or the ladies'?" Hysteria from the audience. I wanted to scream at them to shut up, that right now Charlie was forcing himself to walk through the rain and the dark to find a dead girl. I covered my ears with my hands.

I found the place where Idris had been. She wasn't there. I stood in the drip from the trees, stupefied. Where was she? After the first shock came relief. She hadn't been dead after all. But I'd been so certain. I'd taken lifesaving classes and CPR for months."

I remembered: Charlie and I on the beach one day, giving each other mouth-to-mouth resuscitation, making obscene jokes.

"Why did one lousy lifesaving class make me think I was an expert on what separates life from death? I'd made a mistake, a terrible mistake, because we could have put Idris in the car and taken her to a hospital or to a doctor. But at least I knew now that she was alive when we left."

I stopped reading again and ran my knuckles across my forehead. Charlie! Charlie! She was *dead.* No pulse, Charlie. You were good at lifesaving. You wouldn't make that kind of mistake. Didn't you remember, even for one second, all those old murder mysteries where the body disappears? Didn't you remember how the bad guys come while the hero has gone for the cops and how they remove the evidence? And how the cops stand and ask, "What body? Are you sure there was one? Are you sure you didn't just imagine this?"

Didn't it once occur to you that Idris had died because someone . . . and guess who . . . had given her bad drugs? Drugs that killed her and probably could have been traced back to him? That he'd known where she'd gone to shoot up, into the woods, by the meadow, and when she didn't appear again, he and his friends went looking? And they'd gotten rid of her body.

Oh, it was easy for me to be clever, here, now. I'd seen the note Lon had left. I knew he'd been there when they dropped Idris's body over the Edge of the World. Lon had helped, or watched them do it. But that was impossible for Charlie to imagine.

> I thought she could still be around somewhere, still sick, wandering in circles, too dazed to make her way to the road. There's a cliff at the edge of the high meadow and the minute I remembered that cliff, I panicked. What if she'd stumbled in that direction and fallen?
>
> I ran, shining my light, calling her name. There was no answer except the drift of the rain and the faraway whistle of the Southern Pacific on its way north from LA. I stood at the cliff's edge and played the beam toward the bottom of the drop. It twinkled on broken

glass, shone itself back at me from a rusted fender. And then I began rationalizing again. Idris had been well enough to walk out of here. She'd flagged down a car. Right now she was probably warm in bed, as I should be. Maybe she was telling herself she'd be more careful where she got her stuff from now on. And then I had another thought. Suppose someone came along after we left. Someone more humane, who picked her up and took her to a hospital. That had to be it. Thank God. I decided I *could* forget it. Only Idris knew we'd seen her. And she might not remember, or she might consider us a part of her dreams.

She wasn't in school the next day. I guessed it would take her a day or two to recover or for news of what had happened to get out. She didn't appear the next day either, and I began to have an odd nervous feeling. But I didn't ask if anyone knew anything. The deception had begun.

Idris was never seen again. It was amazing how easily her disappearance was accepted by everyone. Except by her mother . . . and me. Dominique accepted it. "If she wasn't there when you went to look for her, then it's obvious," Dominique said. "She was alive when we left her. She didn't want to come back to Oceanside. She hitched herself a ride just the way everyone says. She's in San Francisco, and you're making way too much of this, Charlie."

Then Idris's mother was making too much of it too. She searched, she asked, she wept. She printed flyers with Idris's picture, and the first time I came face to face with one on the fence by school I almost threw up. I went to see her mother. I didn't know what I would say; I only knew that I had to go. And when I got there, there were no words.

I don't know when I first realized how futile it was for Idris's mother to keep searching. I don't know when

I accepted the fact that Idris was dead after all. One day in that haze of days I admitted that it was so. And then I found something.

I'd been up to the high meadow a dozen times. I couldn't stay away. It was as if that place was the magnet and I was the pin, and wherever I went I felt the pull. Always I stopped at the cliff's edge. But now the pull was downward. I leaned out so far that the slightest breeze could have sent me somersaulting into the void below. And partway down, tangled in a manzanita bush, I saw a limp, red rag. I lay on my stomach and edged myself out as far as I dared, my fingers clutching the tufts of dry grass. The scrap of red was too far for me to reach, but close enough for me to see the golden zodiac signs. I knew what it was. Idris's scarf.

That weekend I went to an area a few miles south of here where you can hike in. It's hard going, but I made it. It took me seven hours.

I smelled her first. Even if you've never smelled death, it's unmistakably terrifying. I made myself go on. And I found what was left of Idris at the bottom of the cliff, hidden from sight by the brush and the clumps of bright yellow wild flowers that I pushed aside with my foot.

I screamed, I remember. Crows rose from the low bushes and circled, screaming with me. I ran. I fell down and retched. I knew that if I lived to be a hundred, I'd never forget Idris and that obscenity of a silver chain and a silver charm around what had once been her throat. I think I had my first suspicion then that I wasn't going to live to be a hundred.

I pushed back my chair and stumbled to my feet, needing to retch myself. You forgot to take off the chain, DD. Bad, careless. A mistake, DD.

There were two more typewritten pages but I couldn't face them, not without air.

I threw open the front door and stood, sucking in deep breaths. A small wind rattled the withered palm fronds. A Fritos bag and a dirty Baby Ruth wrapper blew across the grass. Mrs. Sanchez, her back to me, watered her geraniums. Monday. Harvard was closed Mondays. Mrs. Sanchez's day off. Everything normal. A flight of pigeons shimmered overhead, turning in a flash of silver wings. Charlie's crows, rising, screaming. My chest hurt, and I rubbed it with my fist. Oh, Charlie. What did you do to yourself? What are you doing to me? I made myself go back inside. Gemini man stared at me from the brown envelope, and I traced his outline blindly with my finger before I began again to read.

I told Dominique. I think I scared her when I cried. We were sitting on the blanket out at the beach, because we'd never been back to the high meadow, not since that night. I remember that after a minute Dominique leaned across and wiped my tears away with the flat of her hand.

"You know that I have to tell the police, Dominique," I said. "I can't live with this. I think I'm going mad."

She moved closer and began kissing my face. "Don't, Charlie. Stay out of it. You can't do her any good. You'll destroy yourself . . . and us. You and I, leaving her like that . . ."

I interrupted her. "I can't handle it that she must have been alive. We could have saved her. There's so little difference between life and death. She walked, Dominique, holding that scarf that I took from her head. It was dark. She stumbled to the Edge of the World, and she fell. But we might just as well have pushed her. We killed her. We're responsible."

148

"Oh, don't be so dramatic, Charlie. Whoever gave her the drug killed her. Hysinger, probably. Anyway, she was nothing. Sooner or later, she'd have killed herself. It was only a matter of time."

I pulled away. God . . . I couldn't believe Dominique was saying this. She sounded so heartless. But then I looked down at the sweetness of her face, the softness, and I knew she was saying these things for me.

"You'd lose your scholarship. Wasn't there something in there about high moral character? They wouldn't like this mess. They wouldn't think you acted very morally. And then there's your father, and your mother, Charlie. They're so proud of you. Think of them. Think of me. Sometime, somewhere in this town we must have been seen together. My father will send me away. We'll never see each other again."

I know that stopped me. The thought of losing Dominique.

"You have to put it out of your head, love. You have to."

She tried to make me forget, and sometimes I could. But then I'd look at Idris's poor, broken mother . . . I'd look at Hysinger and his friends who could be selling bad stuff to another girl, killing another one, killing dozens, steadily and slowly, and I couldn't forget. But I couldn't tell either. I considered an anonymous letter. "Look at the bottom of the cliff that borders the high meadow." But Dominique convinced me on that, too.

"Charlie, if you write a note and they find that body, you and I are finished. The police aren't fools. They have experts. They have ways."

There's a time to do what's right, and then the time passes and it's gone forever. For me, it had gone. I began to dream, terrible dreams. I stopped writing poetry because my words frightened me. They sprang from the decay in my soul. When the soul decays, the body dies too. I inspected my body. I looked for skin

149

shriveling, for wounds bleeding. I walked in the darkness of the pit where there was no light and from which I could never escape.

I sat, hunched over, thinking about that pit. I'd been in one just like it myself. Anybody who says he hasn't is either lying, or he has no imagination. I'd fall in there when I'd think too much about my mother dying or about how my father hated me. But the pit days didn't last for me. Something would pull me up and out: A field trip with Noah; Mrs. Sanchez coming over; the thought of Annie. I knew about the pit, though. The pit was bad.

I took a deep breath and went back to Charlie's story.

Dominique was still a part of my life, but I knew she wouldn't be for long. When we were together, I'd pull back. I'd look in her face and see Idris's. Once, with Dominique, I thought I saw maggots around her eyes, and I screamed and tried to rub them away."

I stopped reading again, hurting too much to go on. Why didn't you come to me, Charlie? I would have kept your secret. I'm good with secrets. I could have helped you out of the pit.

But you did come, didn't you? You came, and I was off, ice skating and stopping for hamburgers at Bob's. I had no premonitions.

Duane said I wasn't very sensitive about you. Duane was right.

Dominique was so patient. She'd hold me. She'd tell me to be strong, that everything would be all right. I don't know why she stayed.

You don't know why, Charlie, you big dumb ox? She didn't want you going to the cops. She was nursing you along, trying to keep you sane because she had as much to lose as you did. That wasn't love, Charlie, that was self-protection. Oh, she must have worried plenty, sweet, patient Dominique. What if you blabbed the whole thing? God, the relief it must have been for her when you killed yourself. And then the horror when she found out you'd left a note. Did you blab after all?

One page left. One, and the typing stopped.

Then, last night . . .

He'd meant me to read this on the day he died. By last night he meant Friday night, when he was still alive. What if I'd been home that Saturday? What if he'd given this to me, and I'd read it? Would he still be alive and not in that everlasting darkness?

Then, last night, Dominique and I lay side by side on the blanket, and I was crying again. I've been crying a lot, and Dominique is contemptuous. I can feel it now. She tries to hide it, but I can feel it.

I just bet she tries to hide it, I thought. She can't make you mad at her, Charlie.

We talked about it some more, and she held me and we didn't make love. I couldn't. I don't know if I'll ever be able to again. "Promise me you won't tell, Charlie." I wanted to promise her, but my tongue wouldn't move.

I came home. I can't tell and I can't not tell. One of these days I will tell. Unless I stop myself. So I go to "those silent silver lights and darks undreamed of where I hush and bless myself with silence."

He ended it the way he ended all his stories, with five little dots neatly centered under the last line.

I still had the small white envelope to open. But not yet. A blob of a tear had fallen on the last page I'd read, and I wiped it away with the bottom of my T-shirt. You idiot, Charlie! You and I could have figured this thing out. I'm more suspicious than you. Not so nice. Not so trusting.

Suddenly I was mad, too. Mad at Charlie. So I wasn't there for you. Dammit! Couldn't you have waited one more day? No. You left your story, and then you went home and died for your guilt. A quick snap of the neck and you were gone. I wouldn't have let you do it, Charlie. I wouldn't have let you "bless yourself with silence."

Another blob had mysteriously appeared close to where the first one had been, and I smeared it away. Then I got up, found a paper napkin, blew my nose, and opened the white envelope.

> Dear Jod,
> I can't leave her there for all eternity. I couldn't do the right thing. But you can.
>
> *Charlie*
>
> P.S. I'm sorry about Santa Barbara.

19

I put the pages neatly on top of one another, lining them up, right edge, left edge, top and bottom, the way news-readers on TV do at the end of their half-hour stint. There never in the world was a neater stack of papers. My mind was not neat, though.

Next door "The Phil Donahue Show" was over and the sea "shanty" from a "Gilligan's Island" rerun came on, loud and rollicking. I paced, thinking, talking above the noise.

"You want me to do what's right, Charlie? You know what that's going to mean, don't you? I'd have to go to the police. And I'd have to take this story with me, though I'd hate to, because there's so much in it that I don't want anyone to see . . . not anyone." My voice was choking up on me, and I blew my nose again. "But I'd need it, Charlie. If I went to the police."

I piled the photographs back into their box, careful not to look at them as I put the lid on. And I kept on talking.

"I'd have to go to Lon's mother again, and tell her what the Edge of the World really is, and ask for Lon's note to take with me to the police. She'd need convincing. I'd have to tell her about Idris, and how DD Hysinger may be only one pusher, but he's the one she can help us get. Oh, Charlie! What a can of worms! Are you sure you want me to open it?"

I stopped at the wall calendar and examined it through stinging eyes. It was stuck on January. In the square of the tenth was penciled: Santa Barbara . . . Me and Charlie. We'd gone down, we'd sat in the little patio, the guy at the table next to us had played the harmonica.

"I guess I'll have to call that Rick Pastori," I said. "I need *someone* to share the room. And it won't be the old Gemini men after all." I flipped the pages forward to May. "Some Januaries are gone forever."

A commercial was on next door, and Mr. Yamamoto was using the time to wash dishes. There was the sound of water running, the clatter of plates.

"I don't know what to do, Charlie."

I began pacing again. "If I tell the cops, they'll still be able to find drugs in Idris's body. They'd get the dopers all right. But it would all come out about you and Dominique. There'd be no way to keep that quiet. You know what, Charlie? Dominique wouldn't suffer that much anyway. Her father would just take her away, and she'd be able to comfort herself that she really got him good this time. One in each eye!"

I stood next to the Honda with my hands on the warm leather seat. "God, Charlie! If I *do* tell, so many people are going to suffer." They paraded through my mind: Idris's mother; Lon's mother; Charlie's mom and dad, his sister, Evelyn, and his brother, Dave.

But if I tore the story in little pieces and threw it in the trash, no one would know. Charlie wouldn't know.

I stood by the window, my mind a blank, watching the wind whish the ragged spears of the palm trees against the sky. All of a sudden I thought about the hawk kite, and I knew what I wanted to do.

Annie was home when I called.

"Can I come over, Annie? I have to get the kite."

She didn't seem surprised or ask why. "I'll bring it, Jed," she said, and hung up before I could speak again.

Annie was coming here? I'd never wanted that. But it didn't seem to matter anymore, and in a way it would be good, because more than anything I needed to talk to someone. I needed Annie.

I went to the window to watch for her.

When she came she was on her bicycle, her blue windbreaker puffing out in back on each side of her nylon pack. She stopped at the bottom of our steps, saw me, and waved.

I opened the door. "Hi. Come in."

"Hi." She pushed back her hair, and the wind took it and swept it toward me. As she stepped past me I smelled her clean, sunny, breezy day smell.

I smoothed back her hair and kissed her forehead, and she nuzzled against me.

"I brought it," she said, stepping back and shrugging out of her nylon pack. She laid the golden roll of kite on the table and put the creel of string beside it.

I ran my hand over the smooth silk of the folded feathers.

Annie watched me from the other side of the table. "Something's happened, hasn't it, Jed?"

I nodded. "I want to tell you. I need help to ... no it isn't that." This was hard for me. "Can you stay for a while and ... and just listen?"

Her smile was dazzling. "I can just listen anytime you

want. Anytime." She took my hand and led me to the couch, and we sat close.

It was then I realized that she hadn't once glanced around the room, that she wasn't the least bit interested in this place, only in me. Maybe that's the way it is when someone loves you, I thought. Maybe you don't have to keep that person outside. I knew that this was important, and that I'd need to think about it some more, later. For now, there were other things that were more important.

Annie's eyes never left mine as I told her about Charlie's story and about how he'd found Idris. At first I was able to stay cool the way I usually am and the way I always try to be. But there was a raggedy edge somewhere and I could feel myself unraveling, like a thread being pulled on the edge of a sweater.

"And then he came over here, I guess to talk, and he brought... he brought..." Quicker and quicker the unraveling went, pulling me with it. "But even if I *had* been here... oh, Annie! Do you think he knew that I cared about him? I can't... I don't say things easily. I'm..." A tear ran down my face and I wiped it away, and Annie leaned across and took my wet hand again in both of hers.

"He didn't kill her, you see," I whispered. "But he thought he had. Sometimes thinking you've killed somebody is enough. Especially if you let your guilt grow... as big as the world." My words were fading, and I looked past Annie to my father's old, sagging chair. "It's so easy to let it grow."

She put my hand against her cheek. "Jed? You're shutting me out again."

"I know. I'm trying to stop doing that, too. But Annie ... if I'd been here for Charlie, he might still be alive." My chest hurt so much I could hardly breathe.

156

Annie turned so that we faced each other. "Please listen to me, Jed. If Charlie had wanted to talk to you, he'd have waited. He knew you'd be back. Two minutes! That's how long you said he stayed. Two minutes!"

I got up and ran my hands blindly over the kite.

Annie came and stood behind me. "He could have found you, if he wanted to look. Oceanside's not that big. How many places could you be? Jed? Charlie didn't come to be talked out of what he was going to do. He'd made up his mind. He wanted to leave the story so you'd understand."

The pain in my chest was unbearable.

"It's OK, darling Jed," Annie said softly. "No one's going to mind if you cry."

I couldn't believe the sounds I was making. They were so strange they scared me. "It was the pit," I moaned. "He couldn't get out."

Then Annie put both arms around me, and I was crying and crying as if I'd never stop.

Afterwards, when I stopped shuddering and wiped my eyes, I looked across at the table and saw the hawk, waiting. I still had the hawk.

When Annie left, I rode through the wind and the sun to McCormack Beach. I parked Charlie's bike and stood behind the boathouse to fit the balsa wood struts under the kite. I attached the string then and walked across the sand, the spread of the hawk shivering in my hands. Where the yellow froth bubbled at the sea's edge, I stopped.

"Ready?" I asked, and I wasn't sure if I was talking to the hawk or myself. Or to a friend who might happen to be listening.

I've flown kites since I was a little kid. Usually, even on the breeziest day, you have to run to get the kite up and it will still take a few nosedives before it's truly airborne. Not the hawk.

He rose from my hands, the wind lifting him, and lay on the air between earth and heaven in the same way that real hawks do. I loosened the string and he soared still higher into brightness. Then I pulled the end from the creel and let him go.

Once Charlie and I had stood side by side on this beach. "I am the hawk," he'd said, his face shining in the sun.

Now I was alone here, and I knew that when I'd asked Annie to bring the hawk, and when I'd set it free, I'd been hoping for a miracle. For something to make things right. The hawk would be Charlie, alive again, flying off into light and beauty.

But that couldn't be. Charlie was dead. And death doesn't hand out second chances. This was the final truth; the last letting go. I was crying again, but for the first time since Charlie died, I felt hollowed out and free from pain.

"I won't let it be for nothing, though," I said. "I'm going to the police. Hawk, do you hear me?" I yelled. "I'm going to the police!"

But the hawk had drifted out of sight, and the sky was empty. Charlie's bike — my bike — was waiting. I got on and turned it toward town.